K. SEAN

Kiss of Death

Being with her can be a matter of life and death…

Cover concept by: K. Sean Harris
Cover Design by: Sanya Dockery
Cover Illustration: Courtney Lloyd Robinson
Book Design, Layout & Typesetting by: Sanya Dockery

Published by: Book Fetish

Printed in the U.S.A.   ISBN: 978-976-95303-0-0

*Dedicated to the loving memory of
E. Louise Harris.*

*My love affair with books started
because of you.*

May your soul rest in peace
Love Always.

For her house inclineth unto death, and her paths unto the dead.

Proverbs 2:18

# Chapter 1

Shari looked on, her light brown eyes misty, as Barack and Michelle Obama waved to the record crowd that had attended his inauguration as the 44th President of the United States, as well as the millions of people that were no doubt watching from across the world. She felt proud. She didn't care that a few of her cynical co-workers, especially Danny, the accountant, were cracking jokes at her expense: 'You're acting like you're an American' and 'It's just because Barack is handsome why you're behaving like that'. She couldn't understand how the significance of Obama's meteoric rise could be lost on these educated University graduates. A black family was now occupying the White House. It was nothing short of phenomenal.

She looked on for a moment longer, admiring Michelle Obama's outfit, before heading over to her cubicle to retrieve her Louis Vuitton pocketbook. She had a meeting with the Managing Director of Bolt Communications, the newest player in the local telecommunications industry. Unlike their competitors, Bolt Communications was a Jamaican company, owned by a Jamaican businessman who had made a fortune in the real estate boom in the late 90s. Shari was confident that she would land them as a client. She had prepared a sizzling marketing package for the meeting. She was especially pleased that the managing director was a man. She didn't get along with women very well. For some unknown reason, females always seemed to dislike her on sight. It had always been like that for as long as she could remember. Consequently, she only had two close girlfriends and mostly hung out with guys.

She walked out to the parking lot and hopped into her black 2007 Honda Ridgeline. Shari loved big vehicles. Made her feel safe on the road. It always amused her to see the look on guys' faces when they saw the petite 5'2" beauty exiting or entering the large truck. She had purchased it early last year, using half of the two million dollars that her father had left her to pay down as a deposit. The monthly payment of $60,000 dollars was high but manageable as she earned a good salary and didn't have to worry about rent.

Her father had given her his one bedroom apartment on Haining Road as a graduation present four years ago. A retired veterinarian, he had died two and a half years ago from prostate cancer. She still missed him tremendously. Her dad had been her world. Her parents had gotten divorced nine years ago when she was still in high school and her mother, more out of spite than genuine desire, had taken him to court so that she could have custody of Shari.

Shari exited the parking lot, tooting her horn in greeting to Mr. Sinclair, one of their clients, who had just driven in. Mr. Sinclair owned a health spa and gym and was practically obsessed with Shari. Even after a year of politely spurning his advances, he still would not give up. She liked older guys, but Mr. Sinclair had three strikes against him: he was married, way too old – he was about fifty, and though he was in good shape, wasn't very easy to look at.

She arrived at her destination in fourteen minutes and parked in the sprawling, almost filled to capacity parking lot. Bolt Communications occupied the third floor of the Lexington Marshall Building, the tallest structure on Knutsford Boulevard. She skillfully reversed the large vehicle into a vacant spot between a Toyota Tundra and a Jeep Wrangler. Shari was an excellent driver, her dad had seen to that, giving her lessons from she was twelve years old. She parked and walked briskly inside. She smiled politely at the leering security guard and wrote her name and time of arrival in the guest book. She didn't get offended easily. She had acknowledged the fact a long time ago that men, from all walks of life and of various ages, would always leer at her and try to pick her up so the constant attention, though most of it was unwanted, didn't faze her.

She survived the short elevator ride with two men, a bearer and an executive-looking older man who both had stared at her intensely while she fiddled with her Blackberry, and got off on the 4th floor. She stepped into the offices of Bolt Communications and removed her oversized Dolce & Gabbana sunglasses as she went over to the receptionist.

"Yes? How can I help you?" the receptionist said, her cherry painted lips curled up in an ugly sneer.

Shari was used to unwarranted hostility from women but was still taken aback by the venom in the woman's tone. Then she realized that she knew her. It was Fay. They had attended the same college and in a college full of young, promiscuous girls, Fay had been the biggest slut on campus, which was no easy feat. She had dropped out during her second year after she was caught having sex with three guys in an empty classroom one Friday night. It had been her second time getting caught having sex on the college grounds. This one had received a lot of publicity and embarrassed, the school had decided that enough was enough and asked her to leave. Shari hadn't seen her since. Apparently she had not completed her studies, based on the fact that she was answering phones for a living.

"I have a 2 p.m. meeting with Mr. Pryce," Shari responded, her eyes twinkling with amusement as she remembered some of Fay's notorious antics whilst on campus.

Fay had been accosted and beaten by the daughter of one of the lecturers whom she was sleeping with. The girl, along with two of her friends, attacked Fay and told her to leave her father alone as he was a happily married man. It had been quite a spectacle.

Fay, dragging her envious eyes from Shari's brand new Louis Vuitton pocketbook, made a great show of checking the time on her watch, and seeing that it was exactly 2 p.m., grudgingly buzzed Mr. Pryce on the intercom. Ten seconds later, Shari entered Mr. Pryce's office and closed the door behind her.

"A pleasure to meet you, Mr. Pryce," she said, smiling politely as she attempted, unsuccessfully, to give him a firm handshake. Her tiny hand was swallowed by his mammoth mitt.

"The pleasure is mine, Ms. Golding," he replied in a booming voice, as he held on to her hand a few seconds longer than necessary. "Have a seat."

For the next thirty minutes, Shari skillfully charmed him while deflecting his advances, and in the end, she landed the account. He was very impressed with the campaign that she had in mind but told her that he would only sign the necessary paperwork over dinner. Shari agreed readily enough, having expected him to make a last ditch attempt to get personal, and besides, she knew that he would get nowhere. He wasn't her type and she wasn't one to mix business with pleasure. And last but not least, she was really feeling Nicholas, the guy she was currently dating.

She had met him two months ago at a business seminar and had decided to take a chance with him and see how it goes. It was time to move on. She had still been pining over Daryl, her previous boyfriend, who was murdered a year ago. The shock and pain of losing him aside, his death had really spooked her out. He was the third serious boyfriend she'd had since the age of eighteen that had died a tragic death.

Was something wrong with her? Her friends had done their best to kick that notion to the curb. 'Don't be ridiculous Shari!' they had said, chiding her for actually thinking that she could possibly have had something to do with their deaths. 'It was just a terrible coincidence' they had surmised.

Coincidence or not, it was terrible and more than a bit spooky, that all of her serious boyfriends had passed away under tragic circumstances. First it had been Simon, her first serious boyfriend whom she had been with since her final year in high school. The relationship lasted until four months into her freshman year at college, when he died instantly after being mowed down by a bus as he crossed the street on a busy Friday evening in Cross Roads.

Then there was Teddy, who she had hooked up with several months after Simon's death. He had been of the street variety; rough, rich and used to getting his own way. She had met him at an upscale bar and lounge where she and the girls, feeling for a mature vibe, had gone to knock back a few drinks one Saturday night. Shari, though she knew that he was more than just the legitimate businessman that he claimed he was, dated him anyway and just as she was really beginning to fall in love with him, he was fatally shot in an attempted robbery at one of his business places.

She had taken a nine month break after that until she met Daryl, a dashing forty-three year old University lecturer who helped her tremendously to cope with her father's death. He was stabbed by his secret male lover in a scandalous love triangle gone awry. Shari had had to take a semester off after that one. It had rocked her to the core. Finding out that her boyfriend was a closet homosexual had almost given her a nervous breakdown. And, having him die a violent death like the previous two; was almost too much for her to deal with. Not to mention the nerve-wracking wait for her HIV test results. The word negative had never looked so beautiful. God bless Justine and Yanique, her two closest friends. She would have never recovered without their love and support.

Shari promised Mr. Pryce to call soon to confirm their business dinner, as she ensured to phrase it, and exited his office. She completely ignored Fay as she walked by briskly and went through the glass door.

She thought about Nicholas as she waited with a group of people for the elevator. She was actually planning to give him some tonight. It was time. He had been sweet and patient and there was no reason to hold out any longer. She needed to move on with her personal life and begin to have fun again. She had enjoyed the times he took her out to dinner and the movies, and she had had a blast at the Shaggy charity concert recently. He had impressed her by buying platinum tickets, the most expensive seats in the house. The gifts were thoughtful and lovely too. Orchids, a voucher for the full house treatment at a prominent spa, a motivational book called *Pushing the Envelope: All the Way to the Top,* and a gorgeous Coach tote bag that he had purchased when he went to Miami on a two day business trip.

He certainly knew how to treat a lady.

Tonight she would show him that she knew how to treat a man.

Tonight the ghost of Daryl would be exorcised.
She could feel her vagina becoming moist.
It had been a year since she'd had sex.
Nicholas was in big trouble.

Chapter 2

Nicholas smiled as he ended the call. Tonight was the night. Shari had called to invite him over. She told him that he should come prepared to spend the night. He had just gotten in from the office and was in the living room unwinding to Robin Thicke's latest CD when she called. He checked the time. It was 6:30 p.m. She had not mentioned that she had cooked so he would stop by Mabel's and get some oxtail and beans for dinner. The kind of love making he had planned for Shari could not be conducted on an empty stomach. His stomach growled as if in approval. He got up excitedly to take a quick shower, chuckling at his eagerness. He really liked Shari though. Actually, he was positive that he was in love with her.

In eight short weeks she had had a very positive effect on his life. He was smiling more, had a bounce to his step that hadn't been there since the day he caught Zara, his then girlfriend having sex in his bed with a guy she had introduced early in their relationship as her brother. After everything that he had done for that woman and her family. If he was a different man, he would have been in jail for murder right now. He had been so shocked, so hurt, so devastated that he had thought that he would never recover. But he had. Or at the very least, was well on his way. Thanks to Shari. He showered quickly and got dressed. He then ensured that a pack of condoms was inside his small overnight pouch along with a toothbrush, his special face soap and a moisturizer, and grabbed his keys and headed out. His heart was thudding loudly in anticipation of what the night promised.

CR...ॐCR...ॐ

"Hi Nicholas," Shari purred as she opened the door to her apartment. She was wearing a short, cute lavender silk robe which hinted that she was naked underneath. Her nipples jutted provocatively, straining against the soft fabric.

"Hi Shari," Nicholas replied with a grin as he stepped inside the immaculately kept apartment. Shari was one of the neatest women he had ever come across. Her place was always spotlessly clean and everything was always in order. He kissed her as she closed the door. Her lips were always pouty and soft, and inviting.

"You bought dinner," Shari observed, when they broke the kiss.

"Yeah, you didn't say anything about cooking so I decided to get us something."

Shari chuckled. "I guess I was too caught up thinking about my other hunger..."

She eyed him seductively.

His dick responded immediately.

Shari smiled, took the bag from him and went into the kitchen.

Nicholas sighed and sat down on the comfortable leather sofa. Shari's place was sparsely but impeccably decorated. She didn't like clutter. A marble centre table, a small book stand which housed four rows of books, a black leather sofa, rust-coloured wall to wall carpeting and a 36 inch plasma TV which was mounted on the wall between two large framed photographs of her dad at different stages in his life, were the only things present in the room.

"What would you like to drink?" she called out from the kitchen, which was separated from the living room by a 20 inch counter.

"Fruit punch," Nicholas replied as he looked at the football highlights on the screen. He had never known that a woman as utterly feminine as Shari could love sports so much. The only sport she didn't like as far as he knew was golf, which she merely considered a game and not a sport.

"Ok," Shari replied.

Three minutes later, he was served a steaming plate of oxtail and beans, rice and peas and a tall glass of fruit punch on a tray.

"Thank you, waitress, I'll be sure to give you a large tip," he teased.

"I'm going to hold you to that, sir," she responded with a laugh.

She joined him on the couch with her own tray and they chatted about football while they ate. Shari, being a Liverpool fan, teased him mercilessly about the 2-0 nil defeat his favourite team, Chelsea, had received from Liverpool last Sunday.

They finished eating and Nicholas helped Shari to tidy the kitchen. She couldn't get over how nice he was. She hoped he wouldn't turn out to be *too* nice. Sad as it was, that would eventually bore her. Shari retrieved a bottle of white wine from the refrigerator along with two glasses from the cupboard and led the way to the bedroom.

Nicholas' breathing was ragged as he followed, watching her perfectly round ass perform tricks under the silky material as she strutted sexily. She placed the wine and the glasses on the right bedside table and took up a remote control that was lying on top of the queen-size bed. British songbird Estelle's album *Shine* filtered softly through the surround sound. Shari poured some wine and handed one of the glasses to Nicholas.

"To us," she said softly.

Their glasses clinked lightly and Shari looked at him steadily as she took a sip.

Nicholas could see the passion bubbling in her light brown eyes.

She was ready.

He put his glass down and sat on the bed.

Shari climbed on top of him and sat on his lap, moving her waist slowly on the erection that was crying for freedom from the confines of his jeans.

He groaned and claimed her lips in a deep kiss, their wine-coated tongues dancing to a frenzied up tempo beat.

"Oh Shari...I've wanted you for so long..." Nicholas murmured as she nibbled on his bottom lip and ran her fingers through his extremely curly hair. Nicholas was of Indian descent and she was praying fervently that even if it was true that such men tended to have small dicks, Nicholas would be an exception. He seemed to be slightly mixed so she was keeping her fingers crossed.

Shari, seeing that she had to take charge and speed things up a bit, got up from off his lap and stood in front of him. She untied her robe and shrugged it to the floor. Nicholas' coal-black eyes shone brilliantly in the soft light as he drank in the sight of her luscious body. She was petite yet delightfully curvy; her deceptively wide hips splaying tantalizingly down to her toned, slightly bowed legs. Her fleshy mound, which resembled a juicy peach, filled the wide gap between her legs. It was decorated by a three inch long landing strip just above her protruding clitoris and a silver hoop in the left labia.

Nicholas' dick lurched.

His mouth watered.

"Are you going to sit there and stare all night or are you going to get up and claim this pussy like it belongs to you?" Shari asked saucily with her hands on her hips.

Nicholas rose unsteadily. Shari was so perfect it scared him. A lady on the street and a freak in the bedroom. Independent and childless. Educated and smart. Loved sports. Cute and sexy. What more could a man want?

He hurriedly stripped off his clothes and they tumbled onto the bed. Shari told God a silent thank you. Nicholas' dick, while not exactly a light pole, was a fairly decent size. It would do the trick.

He found her lips again and didn't stop kissing her until he had to come up for air. He then rubbed his lips against her earlobe and nuzzled her arched neck as she caressed his back and whispered nasty things in his ear. It was shocking to hear her speaking like this. He had never even heard her use an expletive before.

She moaned loudly as he worked his way down to her full breasts.

"Oh Nicholas...mmmm...that feels so good," she breathed as he sucked her left breast, twirling the nipple in his mouth as he caressed the right one with his hand. He spent an extended vacation sucking, nibbling and licking them before his tongue travelled down south, leaving a trail of wetness on her washboard stomach.

"Oh fuck!" Shari exclaimed as he licked the inside of her sultry thighs languorously, inching closer and closer to her quivering mound. "Oh God! I can't take it! Ohhhh!"

Nicholas continued to tease her until she was begging him to taste her.

"Please! Please! Please taste my pussy! Nicholas please!" Shari implored, as she writhed beneath his tongue, trying to guide her pussy to his mouth.

It was hot and wet.

It was in dire need of some attention.

Nicholas ended her misery and kissed her pussy like he was kissing her mouth. He pursed his lips against her fleshy mound and slipped his tongue inside as he kissed it forcefully and passionately.

Shari howled with pleasure.

He was going to make her come.

She could feel it building up rapidly as he sucked her mercilessly, the sounds of his oral exertions competing with Estelle's Kanye West assisted song *American Boy*.

"I'm coming Nicholas! Don't fucking stop! Oh God! Oh God! Fuuuck!" Shari shrieked as she clamped Nicholas' head with her thighs, holding it in a tight embrace.

Nicholas moaned as he drank her hot juices thirstily. The dam was broken. Shari thought she wouldn't stop climaxing.

"Sweet mother of Joseph," she murmured in hushed tones as she shivered mightily.

Her first orgasm in a year that wasn't caused by Tickles, her pink vibrator, was a memorable one.

"Mmmm...oh Nicholas...fuck...that was so intense..."

Nicholas grinned.

He was only getting started.

He lowered his head once more.

He licked her labia, twirling her piercing in his mouth before latching on to her turgid clit and sucking it insistently. Shari felt like she was going into cardiac arrest. After such an intense orgasm it was way too soon to be coming again. Try telling that to her ridiculously wet pussy. It pulsed and her clit throbbed as Nicholas wrenched an orgasm from her that made her scream like she was being murdered.

"No...no...Nicholas...I can't take any more...my clit is so swollen it feels like a dick...oh God...no more..." Shari pleaded.

Nicholas had one more trick up his sleeve. Her pleas turned to moans as he licked her clit while he fingered her slowly.

"Mmmm....you fucking bastard...oh shit...you're going to make me come again...you wicked man... you evil fucker...mmmm..."

He slipped in another finger and worked them in a seesaw motion as he continued to lick her trembling clit in a fluid upward motion.

"Oh you motherfucker....I fucking hate you...oh God...Jesus Christ...I hope you drown...I'm coming! I'm coming! I'm coming! Ahhhhhh!"

Shari was delirious. This was the most intense oral assault that anyone had ever launched on her pussy. She whimpered in gratitude when Nicholas finally raised his head.

"You're an evil, evil man," Shari whispered breathlessly.

Nicholas smiled and climbed off the bed. He padded out to the living room to get his pouch. Shari was sitting up on the bed when he returned. He took out the pack of condoms and opened it.

"Not yet," Shari whispered. "I want to taste you..."

He walked over to her and she seized his dick, stroking it gently.

"My turn," she murmured, rubbing it against her lips like it was her new favourite lip gloss before devouring it with her hot mouth.

Nicholas' knees buckled as Shari deep throated him effortlessly.

"Shari...ahhhh....damn..." he moaned as his shaft disappeared down her throat over and over again.

She played with his testicles as she concentrated on the tip, pursing her lips and sucking it insistently, giving him a taste of his own medicine.

Too good a taste apparently.

She could feel his scrotum tightening and his dick throbbing.

He was getting ready to climax.

Hell no, not yet.

She removed his dick from her mouth with a loud plop and pressed a solitary finger down hard just below his scrotum. His dick trembled in confusion as his climax made a U-turn.

Nicholas looked at Shari in wonder. Where the hell did she learn to give head like that?

"Put that condom on and violate my pussy," Shari instructed.

Nicholas growled and in his haste, ripped the condom. He quickly got out another one and rolled it on. Shari braced herself on her elbows and he tucked her legs way back and entered her slowly, burying it to the hilt.

"Yessss....fuck yeah...give me all of it..." Shari implored, as she maintained eye contact.

The look on Nicholas' face was one of pure bliss. He was in heaven.

"Mmmm...inside you feels so good...so hot and sweet..."

"Shut up and fuck me! Fuck me hard Nicholas! Tear this pussy up!" Shari growled.

Nicholas attempted to rise to the challenge. He pulled her closer to the edge of the bed and clutched her close to him as he drilled her mercilessly, his testicles slapping her thighs with each ferocious thrust.

"I'm a big girl! I'm a big girl! I'm a big girl! Fuck me! I want my pussy to ache all day tomorrow!"

Nicholas couldn't take it. He fucked her at the speed of light as he could feel his orgasm rushing back to the fore with a vengeance.

Shari felt it too.

"Stop! Don't move! Don't you dare fucking move!" Shari shouted.

Nicholas was still, except for his legs. They were shaking badly. He felt faint. His orgasm teetered at the point of no return before reluctantly retreating.

Shari gestured for him to pull out. He did so. She then commanded him to lie on his back and got on top of him. She slid down his shaft until it was completely buried inside her. She then gyrated and moved her waistline in a circular motion as she went up and down his shaft.

"Oh God Shari...you feel so good baby...so good...ahhhh....mmmm....Christ..."

"You like my pussy Nicholas? Huh? You like my fat, sweet pussy? Huh?"

"Yes Shari! I love it! I love it baby!" Nicholas proclaimed passionately as Shari bounced up and down his shaft rapidly, willing his throbbing dick to make her come again.

Nicholas lost it. He grabbed Shari's ass cheeks and held her in mid-air, thrusting upwards like his life depended on it.

"Yes! Give it to me! Break it off inside me! Make me come again!" Shari screamed as Nicholas, with his face a snarling, unrecognizable mask, fucked her with everything he had.

They climaxed mere seconds apart.

Their grunts, screams and moans sounded inhumane.

"I love you Shari," Nicholas said softly as they lay beside each other spent.

Shari didn't know what to say, so she said nothing.

After a prolonged silence she heard light snoring.

Turned out she didn't have to respond.

Nicholas had fallen asleep.

The condom was still on his flaccid dick.

Shari removed it and disposed of it in the bathroom. She then cleaned his dick with a wash cloth and got another sheet to cover with. There was no way she could move him to get underneath the covers.

Shari sighed contentedly.

God she had needed that.

The sex had been good.

Real good.

She fell asleep with a smile on her face.

hapter 3

Three days later, the following Friday, Shari was heading back to the office from a power lunch with a prospective client when her mobile rang. Keeping her eye on the slow-moving traffic on Knutsford Boulevard, she rummaged through her tote bag and fished out her Blackberry. It slipped from her hand as she brought it to her ear and fell at her feet. She bent down to quickly retrieve it, only to feel the truck bump into something. Cursing, she grabbed the phone and raised her head. She had hit somebody's car.

The person, a tall guy with a scowl on his handsome face, had already alighted and was walking towards the back of his vehicle to inspect the damage.

Shit! Shari fumed as she got out of her truck. Just what she needed. A fender bender in the grueling Friday afternoon traffic. The light had changed to green and the vehicles in her lane began blowing incessantly. She sighed and went to look at the damage. Her eyes bulged in shock. How the hell could that little nudge have caused so much damage? The trunk of the guy's car was badly dented and the taillights on both sides were broken.

"Hi," Shari said to him. "Sorry about this but don't worry, I'll have it fixed quickly. I'd also appreciate if we could deal with this without getting the police and the insurance company involved."

He looked away from his beloved Honda Accord coupe and looked down at the short, attractive, well-dressed woman. She was young, didn't look a day over twenty. He was pissed about the car but at least he didn't have to deal with some asshole who would try to pull a fast one. This was a nice professional looking young lady who most likely would be true to her word.

"I'm listening," he drawled lazily, as though he was on a beach somewhere relaxing and not standing up in the ripe Friday afternoon sun dealing with a care-less driver.

"I have a very reputable mechanic who operates on Old Hope Road. You can take it there tomorrow to have the damage assessed after which it would be repaired sometime next week," Shari told him, all business. Though the guy was disturbingly hot, she was surprised to find herself attracted to him. Usually when she was in a relationship, other men, regardless of how they looked and what they had didn't get her attention. And she also wasn't usually attracted to young guys. He looked to be about twenty-five. She liked her men thirty-five years old and older. She shrugged aside the irrelevant thoughts and focused on the matter at hand.

"Let's pull over on Antigua Boulevard," he suggested, looking back at the cars that were trying to cross over to the next lane. "We're blocking up the traffic."

Shari nodded and climbed back into her vehicle. She looked at the back of his car as she drove behind him onto Antigua Boulevard. This little indiscretion was going to cost her a pretty penny. Good thing she could afford it. He pulled over in front of a brokerage firm and she parked behind him.

She stayed in her vehicle this time. He sauntered over and bent down slightly by the window. She got a whiff of his cologne. A very masculine and sexy scent that she was not familiar with.

"Ok, we can do that," he said, picking up where they had left off.

Damn he has nice teeth, Shari noticed.

"Here's my information," she said, handing him an embossed business card. "I'll call the mechanic in a little while to let him know you'll be coming to see him. What time should he expect you?"

He looked at the card before responding. She was an advertising and marketing executive. Maybe he could utilize her services one of these days. Get some real marketing going for his young, but growing business.

"About 10 in the morning," he replied, handing her a card of his own.

She examined it. Karim Dawkins. CEO of Mobile Clean, a mobile car wash and detailing business. A young entrepreneur. Good for him.

"Ok, so we'll be in touch, and sorry for the inconvenience." She gave him a brief smile and gunned her engine.

"Bye and be careful on the road," he said, wanting to say much more but instinctively knew that Shari wasn't the type to get picked up by men on the road. Well he had her digits, perhaps another time, in another setting, he would make a move.

"Thanks, but I usually am," she replied with a smirk. Karim moved out of the way and she headed down the street, taking the right turn onto Barbados Avenue. Karim then got into his car and headed to his office, which was located at an industrial park on the outskirts of New Kingston. He was also a silent partner in a car dealership located on Ripon Road and he also had a clothing line called Vanguard Designs which specialized in graphic T-shirts for men and women. His close friend in Miami, Taj, where the business operated from, handled the designing end of things. The line was popular in Miami, and rising rap star Lioness, a Jamaican born rapper who fused her music with reggae, was a big fan of the line. The T-shirts were also popular with the uptown crowd in Kingston, and Karim would often see people wearing them at the uptown parties.

He thought about Shari as he waited for the security guard to open the gate to the industrial park. She had made quite an impression on him. He was impressed by the way she had handled the situation. She was very cute and sexy. Her fitted black slacks and cute red vest worn over a black shirt had done little to hide her luscious curves.

He was trying to cool down and find a nice girl to settle down with. He was a very busy man and having multiple women was getting to be very taxing. Of all the women he was currently dating, Kimberly was probably the one he fancied the most but he didn't see a future with her. Kimberly was hot, sexy and smart, but she was lazy. All she wanted to do was dress up all the time and be seen at all the hot spots. Fancied herself a young, upcoming socialite. Karim didn't like that. He wanted an independent, hardworking woman. Someone who could help him to make money, not spend all of his. He wondered if Shari was that kind of woman.

He parked in his spot and went inside. Aiesha, his receptionist and personal assistant, was dealing with a customer. He went into his office and closed the door. He switched on his Mac and checked his email. Taj had emailed four new designs for him to look at. He forced Shari to the recesses of his mind and opened the first picture.

CR...SOCR...SO

"Hi babe," Shari said to Nicholas, a few hours later. He had called to find out if she had already left the office. They were going to the movies to see Notorious, the Biggie Smalls biopic. "I'm leaving out right now."

Nicolas sighed. He hated going to the movies late and at this rate, the only way Shari would make it on time was if she took a helicopter.

"Don't be pissed, I couldn't leave any sooner honey," Shari said soothingly. "Matter of fact, tell you what, go ahead and get the tickets for the 8:30 showing instead. That way we'll make it on time."

"Ok," he agreed, after a pregnant pause. "I'll pick you up at 8."

"Great, see you later boo."

She then hung up and made her way out to the parking lot. Things were going great with her and Nicholas though sometimes he was too much of a softie. She had to make a conscious effort not to take advantage of his mild mannered ways. When Nicholas was displeased about something, all he did was sigh and pout. Sometimes Shari found it cute but other times downright disgusting. He needed to grow a backbone, be a *man*. Teddy, her third boyfriend, had been the opposite. He had been a very masculine, take charge kind of guy. She had really loved that. But Nicholas was a good man. Good in bed, loving, kind and affectionate. That works too. But sometimes, just sometimes, his softness grated on her nerves.

ѻ…ѡѻ…ѡ

"Mmmm…I missed this dick…yes Karim…fuck me!" Aiesha moaned as Karim fucked her from behind. They were in his office where she was bent over his desk, with her black pleated skirt bunched up around her waist and her black thong pulled to the side. One evening, two weeks after she had gotten the job six months ago, she had mustered up the courage to tell her young boss that he could have her anytime he wanted, with no strings attached. He had been amused by her declaration and had not taken her up on the offer until one Friday evening, fifteen minutes after closing time, she had knocked on his office door and entered the room stark naked. One look at her smooth, thick, nude body made him throw caution to the wind. He didn't think it was a good idea to have intimate relations with an employee but he had yet to regret it. She had given him a very satisfying fuck in the same position she was in now. They had had sex several times after that, but not in the past three weeks.

"Yes boss...almost there...just like that," she groaned as she got ready to climax for the second time. Getting it good from behind always made her come. Hard. "Yes! Yesss! Yesss! Its right there! Ahhhhh!"

Karim watched her voluptuous ass jiggle as she climaxed. He continued to stroke her deep and hard, loving the way her juices threatened to wash the condom from off his dick. Aiesha was built for sex. Thick, sensuous thighs; a plump ass that bounced delightfully even when she just breathed and large breasts that despite their size, were very firm. She was also very freaky. There was very little that she hadn't done to him sexually. What he really respected about her though, was that she displayed a level of maturity way beyond her twenty years. Outside of their sexual rendezvous, she always referred to him as Mr. Dawkins and always behaved appropriately. No one could ever come by the office and deduce that he was sleeping with her based on how they interacted with each other. She did her job well and was a big hit with their customers. They loved the pleasant, attractive young woman who always had a joke or kind word. She was a real people person and an asset to his business. Karim considered himself lucky to have her.

"Give me one more before you come boss...just one more...juice this pussy one more time..." she moaned, spreading her legs wider and putting her hands on the floor.

Karim groaned. When she gave it to him like this it drove him wild. His thrusts became less controlled as he increased his tempo. He slapped her ass cheeks viciously. Just the way she liked it.

"Ahhh! Yes boss! Fuck mi pussy til it shift outta position! Oh God! Yes! Give it to me! Don't stop! Coming again!"

Karim gritted his teeth as he tried to make her climax before he did. The race was on. His toes were curling in the confines of his Kenneth Cole loafers. He was almost there. He stuck his left index finger in her winking anus as he slung his right leg on top of his desk, kicking over his fourteen carat gold pen holder, and really dug down deep inside her.

Aiesha howled like a woman possessed.

"Fuck!" she shrieked as she climaxed, collapsing to the floor with Karim still inside her. They positioned sideways and he squeezed her nipples as he went for the prize. Aiesha raised one thick leg in the air to give him more leverage.

"Come for me boss! Let it out! Release the bloodclaat juice!" she urged wantonly.

"Ughh! Uggh! Arggghh!" Karim grunted unintelligibly as he spilled his seed inside the lubricated condom.

He pulled out of her and lay on his back, looking up at the ceiling as the aftershocks made him shudder like he was freezing.

The weekend was off to a great start.

Chapter 4

"The movie was really good," Nicholas admitted grudgingly, as they headed towards his home. Not being a hip hop fan, he had been skeptical about going to see a movie about a rapper, whether or not that rapper had been one of the best rappers ever. But it had been a very enjoyable movie; sad, but enjoyable. He was going to purchase the two albums that the young man had managed to record before his untimely death and get acquainted with his music.

"Yeah, it was," Shari agreed. Better than she had thought it would be. She was especially pleased with the performance of the actress who played the role of Lil Kim. She had done an excellent job. She wondered when they would do a movie about Tupac Shakur. There have been numerous documentaries about his fascinating life but no movie.

The spicy aroma of the pound of jerk pork on the backseat assaulted Shari's nostrils mercilessly. She couldn't wait to dig in to it. After the movies, Nicholas had stopped by the jerk centre on Holborn Road to get jerk pork.

They got to Nicholas' two bedroom apartment in Beverly Hills and Shari went straight into the bedroom to change into one of Nicholas' button down shirts. He came out of the kitchen to find her rooted in front of the T.V. watching the Los Angeles Lakers take on the Detroit Pistons. She was a Lakers' fan but she loved Allen Iverson. She watched as he dismissed a defender with his signature crossover dribble and nailed a fifteen foot jumper from the right side of the court, stretching Detroit's slim lead to four points.

"Oh babe, I forgot to tell you...I had a minor accident today," Shari told him as she took the plate with jerk pork and festival from Nicholas' outstretched hand.

Nicholas' eyes bulged. "Really? Where? How?"

Shari grinned at his reaction. "Calm down babe...it was just a little fender bender. Happened on Trafalgar Road this afternoon. I ran into the back of some guy's car."

"How did that happen? He stopped suddenly?"

Shari chewed a piece of the succulent pork and watched Kobe Bryant deliver a thunderous dunk over a hapless defender that brought the capacity crowd to its feet before responding.

"No, my cell phone fell and by the time I picked it up I had hit his car," she told him nonchalantly.

He looked at her incredulously. "That's unlike you...being so careless. How bad is the damage?"

"Don't worry about it," Shari snapped. Shit she already knew she was at fault, she didn't need to hear it again.

"I'm sorry babe but I was just saying..."

"Its no big deal Nicholas...just drop it, yeah?" Shari told him without taking her eye off the screen.

"I'll pay for the damage," he offered, trying to make peace. He hated when Shari was upset with him. "How much is it?"

"Are you deaf?" Shari queried, then immediately felt bad for being rude when she saw the embarrassed and hurt look on his face.

She kissed him on the cheek.

"I'm sorry for saying that...but I'm a bit testy about the incident. It was very uncharacteristic of me. I'll find out what it's going to cost tomorrow."

"Its ok honey, I understand. Ok, just deal with it and bring the bill to me," he declared.

"Ok babe, you're such a sweetheart," Shari told him truthfully. Nicholas was without a doubt one of the sweetest persons she had ever met. She shuddered to think what would happen to him if he had had a girlfriend like her best friend Justine. Justine did not play when it came to money. Any man that she dated had to have heavy pockets and light hands. Justine loved money so much that Shari swore she must have been a Jew in her former life. But then again, Nicholas' ex-girlfriend, Zara, was a money hungry user who had almost brought him to his knees emotionally and financially before she decided that he had served his purpose and moved on. So he knew what it was like.

They ate and watched the game in a mostly comfortable silence, broken occasionally by Shari's excited utterances every time she saw a good play.

Nicholas watched her more than he watched the game. He loved her so much. He was positive that she would be his wife one day in the not too distant future. He was thirty-nine years old. Would be forty in June. He wasn't getting any younger. He didn't want to scare her though, so he would give it some more time before he broached the subject of marriage. He placed the empty plates in the kitchen sink and came back to cuddle with her on the couch. He was so relaxed and comfortable that he fell asleep before halftime.

CR...ЅꙬCR...Ѕꙩ

Zara sipped her red wine thoughtfully. She was at Illusion, a lounge and bar favoured by diplomats, politicians and connected businessmen with her man of the moment, a fifty year old investor from Canada with deep pockets, but she was preoccupied. They had stopped by the jerk centre on Holborn Road to get jerk pork earlier and she had seen Nicholas there with a pretty young thing. He hadn't seen her as they had already made their purchase and was in the SUV getting ready to leave.

He had looked so carefree and *happy.*

And in love.

He had looked nothing like the broken down pathetic wimp that she had discarded like a piece of rubbish eight months ago. Apparently he had picked himself up, dusted himself off and recharged his batteries. He looked good too. He had the kind of glow a man had when he was very comfortable and happy with his life. She didn't like it. He should still be missing her. Still be miserable and heartbroken. She looked over at Arthur. He was talking to her about the stupid stock market but she was only half hearing him. She decided she would give Nicholas a call soon or even better, pay him a visit. After his initial shock she was sure that he would be happy to see her. After all, it was a female trait to hold grudges.

CR…SOCR…SO

Nicholas smiled and moaned. He was having a really good erotic dream. He was lying on his back and Shari was pleasuring him with her hot, knowledgeable mouth. She was sucking him languidly, almost worshipfully, as she wrapped her nimble tongue around his member and took him in deeply and slowly, over and over again. It was so good that he didn't want to wake up. She massaged his scrotum and played with his testicles as they tightened in her grasp. His toes stiffened unnaturally as she coaxed his orgasm to the fore. It seemed to be crawling towards his dick from every part of his body. He felt tingly all over and his heart clanged against his chest as his heart beat accelerated. The dream felt so real.

Oh God, he was about to blow.

No, not yet.

He didn't want it to end.

He didn't want to wake up.

He grunted hoarsely as he erupted in her mouth.

She swallowed every drop.

He opened his eyes.

She was sitting on her knees in front of him, wearing a devilish, semen-stained smile.

"About time you woke up," she commented wryly.

Nicholas laughed heartily. "Damn...I thought I was dreaming. That was crazy...*you're* crazy..."

"You have no idea..." Shari teased as she turned the T.V. off. It was now 1:25 a.m. The game, the second of a double header, had finished fifteen minutes ago.

She had been sucking him off in his sleep since the final whistle.

"C'mon," Shari said, getting up. "Let's go to bed."

From the look in her eyes and her husky tone, Nicholas knew that they weren't going there to sleep.

He was right.

Chapter 5

"**Y**eah! Wicked play!" Shari cheered through a mouthful of hot wings. She was at a popular restaurant and sports bar watching the Super Bowl. She was rooting for the underdog Cardinals. They had just scored a touchdown. Justine and Yanique, her two best friends, were there with her though their only interest was watching all those sweaty, muscular men running around in tights.

"Look at his bulge!" Justine commented enthusiastically, referring to one of the linebackers.

"Yeah, he's holding," Shari agreed. The guy reminded her of Teddy, her third boyfriend. Tall and heavy. Teddy had been 6 feet tall and weighed 285 pounds. Whenever they had sex, she was usually on top. She had always felt like a moth fucking an elephant. The girls used to tease her mercilessly. 'How you manage him Shari?' and 'Shari you're a brave girl!'

She used to just laugh. She had managed Teddy just fine. His dick was just as big as the rest of him but she had handled it with much aplomb. She was a small girl, only 5' 2", but when it came to vehicles and dicks, as far as she was concerned, the bigger the better.

She glanced at her two friends, who were now busy scrutinizing the four guys and one girl who were sitting several tables away. She had been friends with Yanique since high school and they had both met Justine in their freshman year at college. The three of them, though very different in a number of ways, had been inseparable since. Shari was the beautiful, fun though level-headed one, very focused and career driven. Yanique was a tall, thick mulatto who treated sex like it was a sport, and who had anger management issues; she was the warrior of the crew.

She worked in the personal banking section of Jamaica's largest commercial bank. Shari wondered everyday how she had kept that job for so long until Yanique had confessed that she was fucking her married female boss and as such got away with murder in the department. Justine was tall and slender, and considered herself the fashionista of the crew though they all knew that none of them had as much style and fashion sense as Shari. She used to dabble in modeling for a few years but was now an accountant at one of Kingston's major hotels. She had a competitive streak that got on the other two girls' nerves at times but they loved her like a sister nevertheless.

Shari looked over at the table. She recognized the one they were 'ooohing' and 'aaahing' about. It was the guy whose car she had hit. They had spoken yesterday, when he called after leaving the mechanic's shop. It was going to cost fifty-eight thousand dollars to repair his car. Shari had assured him that his car would be good as new and ready for pick up on Wednesday as long as he took it to the mechanic early Tuesday morning. Their eyes met across the room and he nodded to her almost imperceptibly.

She nodded back a greeting. He looked delicious, sitting over there at ease with his friends, enjoying the game. He was wearing a striped Polo shirt which hugged his athletic frame, but not too tightly. Both of his ears sported a diamond knob. Well, her business with him was done. There was no reason for them to ever speak again. She hoped she didn't keep bumping into him around town. She smiled at the pun and quickly averted her face just in case he thought that she was smiling at him.

"You know him Shari?" Justine asked suspiciously. She never missed anything.

"Yeah, it was *his* car I damaged the other day," Shari replied casually.

"For real? That's one *fine* negro," Justine said, looking at him hungrily. "He can put these long legs on his shoulders anytime."

Yanique chuckled in agreement. "You're right about that."

Shari looked at Yanique with mock cynicism. "There's no way on the earth the poor guy could manage your tree trunks on his shoulder Yanique."

Yanique fumed as Shari and Justine cackled.

"Men *love* my juicy, voluptuous body... so shut up and watch the game," was the best comeback she could think of.

Shari chuckled triumphantly and turned her attention back to the game. The boring half-time show was over. It was time for the game to resume.

CR...SOCR...SO

Karim sipped his beer and half-listened to Ramona as she told them about a female newspaper vendor who was sexually assaulted by a man of unsound mind on the streets of Montego Bay in broad daylight. He was trying to put into perspective the butterflies he had felt in his stomach when he spoke to Shari yesterday and when he laid eyes on her just now. Was it possible for a twenty-six year old man to have a crush? He didn't think so. Then what was it? An intense liking though he barely knew her? The excitement of a new piece of quality ass? No, that wasn't it. Yeah he was attracted to her physically but there was more to it. There was just something about her that he found irresistible. What was he going to do about it?

Chapter 6

"Hello?" Nicholas said when he answered the call. He was heading home after visiting his mom for the evening when his iPhone vibrated in his pocket. It was an unknown number.

"Hi Nicky," a sultry voice purred.

He almost lost control of the vehicle. It couldn't be. *Zara!* Why was she calling him? What the fuck did she want? All the hurt, pain and embarrassment he had felt at her soft, manicured hands that he had thought were buried returned from the dead with full force.

"It's me, Zara," she told him, knowing fully well that he knew who it was. "How are you?"

Nicholas had trouble breathing much less speaking. His throat felt tight, reminding him of that courtroom scene in *The Devil's Advocate*. He coughed for several seconds until it finally subsided. He turned off the AC and put the windows down. He took a deep breath.

"Are you ok?" she asked.

"What do you want?" he asked hoarsely, not bothering to hide the hostility in his voice.

"I've been thinking about you for a long time now," she responded. "And I wanted to call but didn't have the courage to...before now."

It sounded as though she was crying.

"I left you on really bad terms and I wanted to apologize for the way I hurt you. I've never stopped loving you Nicky...despite the way I acted and all the terrible things that I did to you...I never stopped loving you."

Nicholas was silent. He pulled over and leaned back in his seat. His vision was blurry. There were tears in his eyes. He remembered that day when he had gotten home early to find the man whom he thought was her brother, fucking her with wild abandon in his bed, and the contemptuous sneer she had on her face when she saw that he had caught her in the act. He remembered the money he had given her for what he thought was for a doctor bill for her sister when she had been hospitalized for ulcer problems only to discover, after overhearing a telephone conversation, that it was used to pay for an abortion and to buy designer clothes for her 'brother'.

Love. That word was blasphemous coming from Zara's mouth. He felt embarrassed and ashamed at the way he had allowed himself to be used and abused.

"You never loved me," he said tightly. "You have no idea what it is like to love someone other than yourself. I've moved on and I'm happy. Do. Not. Call. Me. Again. Ever."

Zara was surprised at his words and the subsequent dial tone. *So little Nicky has some balls now,* she thought in amusement. Perhaps he was just shocked to hear from her and was grappling with the bad memories. But she would not be deterred. She would re-enter his life and crush him like a bug. And this time, when she was through with him, there would be nothing left of his soul.

CR...SOCR...SO

"Baby what's wrong?" Shari queried. She was home now, getting ready for bed. After the game, which the Cardinals had lost much to her chagrin, she hung out with the girls for a couple more hours, drinking and chatting. She was tired now and needed to get some rest. Tomorrow was Monday and she loved to start the work week right. She had called Nicholas to have a quick chat with him before she fell asleep.

"Zara called me earlier tonight," he told her.

"Your ex? What the hell did *she* want?" Shari asked, surprised.

He told her about the brief conversation.

"That's really odd that she would call out of the blue like that," Shari remarked. "But don't let it get to you baby...you're fine now...you have someone who appreciates you and genuinely cares about you. Fuck that bitch. She's not even worth a thought."

He noticed that she didn't say love. Shari didn't love him. Yet. He couldn't wait for the day that she would look him in the face and utter those three little words. He was a romantic at heart. And it was important to him for the woman he loved to love him in return. But he would wait. God knows she was worth it.

"Thanks baby," he sniffed.

Shari knew that he had been through a lot with that witch and she was sorry for him but she had to get off the phone. She couldn't bear to hear a grown man crying. Especially because of a woman that was not a member of his family. The death of a mother or grand-mother; that she could understand. Or even a sister or a close aunt but this was ridiculous to say the least.

"Ok, honey, I'm going to bed now. I have a slight headache and I have to be up early tomorrow," she told him. "Sleep tight, ok?"

"Goodnight baby, I love you."

"Goodnight honey."

Shari hung up and climbed into bed. Nicholas really needed to man up. His ex called and he was over there crying like a little bitch. She sighed and pulled the covers over her head. Maybe that was what was preventing her from really falling in love with him. Everything else was perfect but she just couldn't get over the fact that he was as soft as cotton candy. She fell asleep wondering what Zara looked like.

# Chapter 7

The following Wednesday, Karim went to pick up his car at the mechanic in the early afternoon. He looked it over. The mechanic had done a good job. He drove out feeling satisfied and decided to give Shari a call. There was no need for him to call her but he wanted to. He dialed her number as he waited at the red light. He turned on the AC and put his windows up to block out the loud music coming from an over packed, decrepit taxi in the adjacent lane.

Shari answered on the fourth ring.

"Hello, good afternoon," she said, sounding a bit harried.

"Hi, Shari, this is Karim Dawkins," he said.

"Oh, hi, is everything ok with the car?"

"Yeah, its fine, I was just calling to let you know."

"Ok thanks, that's great. I'm a bit busy so I have to go but take care of yourself," Shari told him. She really was busy but she didn't like the way she felt whenever she heard his voice. It had happened on Saturday as well when he had called. It was very disconcerting.

"Ok, you too."

Karim hung up and slipped his Blackberry inside the holster on his waist. So that was that. He doubted he would ever call her again. It was obvious that she didn't like him or was the kind of woman that liked for men to sweat her. No use in getting himself caught up chasing a chick that wasn't into him. He would be playing himself.

CR…SOCR…SO

Later that night, Shari decided to stop by Nicholas' apartment before heading home. She hadn't seen him since Sunday and it seemed as though he was still moping about the call he had gotten from his ex. It was 8 p.m. and she was just leaving the office. Today had been a long day, matter of fact it had been a hectic week. There was a recession but people still needed to advertise and get their products out there, and for those in the know, having Shari Golding handle your account would ensure that you got the most bang for your buck. Some of the other employees hated on Shari but the boss knew where his bread was buttered so he handled her with kid gloves. Shari bought in 45% of the company's advertising business. That was nothing he could afford to scoff at. So she pretty much was left up to her own devices to a certain extent. Nicholas was already home when she called to let him know that she would be coming to see him.

She got there in fifteen minutes and parked behind his forest green Mitsubishi Grandis. Shari didn't like his vehicle. It was a family vehicle, the kind a man drove when he had a wife and three kids. Nicholas had a family but his ex-wife – they had been divorced for six years – and his five year old son lived in Montreal with her new husband. He rarely got to see the child and truth be told, his son didn't seem to mind as he and his step-father got along really well. Shari called him to let him know that she had arrived and he opened the door. He had offered her a key to his apartment the other day but she didn't accept it. There was no need for her to have a key to his place.

"Hey you," she said and hugged him before walking pass and going to sit down on the couch.

He closed the door and joined her on the couch. Shari looked at the T.V. She was appalled to see it on the Lifetime channel. What the fuck was wrong with Nicholas?

She looked at him, unable to hide her annoyance.

"You watch *Lifetime*?" she asked incredulously.

"Yeah, some really good movies come on Lifetime," he responded with a serious expression.

Shari took a deep breath. She was just about to tell him that she had only stopped by for a brief visit when there was a knock on the front door.

Nicholas, his face scrunched up in surprise, got up to see who it was.

"Jesus Christ! What are you doing here?" Shari heard Nicholas exclaim. He stepped outside and pulled the door shut but she could still hear him.

"Are you crazy Zara? You can't just show up at my house like this!"

Shari had heard enough. There was no way she was sticking around to deal with this crap. Nicholas had better grow some hair on his balls and deal with this shit soon. If it was a case where he had a crazy ex who just couldn't get it in her head that the relationship was over, she would look at the situation differently and help him deal with it but this was happening simply because Nicholas refused to stand up and be a man. She got up and opened the door. They were standing beside his vehicle talking in hushed tones. He turned around and saw her.

"Umm...Shari this is Zara, Zara this is Shari my girlfriend...she came by unexpectedly babe and she was just leaving," Nicholas said nervously. He didn't know what to do. Zara was arguing with him instead of leaving and now Shari looked like she was leaving. Fuck! He really hated confrontations.

Shari couldn't believe the nerve of this idiot. Her face a mask of incredulity, she walked pass the two of them and hopped into her truck.

"Shari, Shari, wait!" Nicholas called out, sprinting towards her vehicle.

She ignored him and headed out. She couldn't believe such a sweet, nice man could be so unbelievably spineless and stupid.

CR...℘CR...℘

"Look at the trouble you've caused!" Nicholas said miserably. "Why you couldn't just leave? Eh?"

"I'm sorry Nicky," Zara said soothingly. "I just had to see you...I'm not sleeping well at night knowing how things ended between us...its really affecting me in a bad way...I just had to come and see you to try and explain...ask for your forgiveness..."

Nicholas looked in her tear-filled eyes. Seven months after the fact. It was too little too late. He was happy now, had moved on with his life. This was a disruption he did not need or want. Zara could be very unpredictable and persistent though. He decided to take the conciliatory route.

"Look its over now...whatever happened is in the past...we've both moved on...I harbour no hard feelings...ok?"

She smiled through her tears.

He remembered how that smile used to have the ability to make his day.

She hugged him unexpectedly. He could feel the swell of her 36 DDs against his chest. His heartbeat accelerated to what he was sure was unsafe territory. She hugged him tighter and he could feel his body responding. It amazed him that after everything that he had been through with her that she could still arouse him, especially this easily.

"Zara..." he began, and tried to gently extricate himself from her embrace.

Plump lips reached up and stopped him in mid-sentence, her tongue darting inside his open mouth.

His mind was telling him that this was wrong, that this should not be happening, but his body was reacting fiercely, acting on its own accord, giving in to the sensations that were pricking it all over.

She moaned in his mouth and subtly ground her pelvis against his turgid erection which had turned his plaid house shorts into a tent. She reached down and rubbed it through his shorts as she deepened the kiss, making his knees weak with passion. Zara broke the kiss, and still holding on to his dick, led him inside. Nicholas followed meekly, his brain a confused mess with his body feeling detached from it, as though he was merely an observer of what was happening. They reached inside and she closed the door.

CR...SOCR...SO

Shari got home and headed straight to the bathroom where she took a quick shower. She was so disgusted with Nicholas that she wanted to puke. So that was the famous Zara. She wasn't pretty but her brown angular face and thick pouty lips had an attractive quality about it. Her breasts were huge and admittedly, she had a nice body. Tall and slightly thick with a curvy shape. She stepped out of the shower and dried herself. She wondered what was going to happen now. She liked Nicholas but tonight was the final straw. When he called her, and she was surprised that he wasn't ringing off her phone yet, she would give him an ultimatum. Either he started acting like a man and get his act together or he could continue behaving like the punk of the century all by his lonesome, or with his demonic ex, whichever he preferred, but she would not put up with it anymore. That settled, she lathered her skin with her favourite body crème and climbed into bed. She turned the T.V. on and put it on the soccer channel. She wasn't even hungry though she hadn't eaten all evening. Nicholas had spoiled her appetite.

CR...SOCR...SO

"You know you missed me Nicky...didn't you baby? Huh? You missed your pussy didn't you baby?" Zara purred as she slowly bounced up and down Nicholas' shaft. They hadn't made it further than the door. Once she had locked the door, Zara had pounced on him, stripping off his clothes and kissing and caressing him everywhere in a passionate frenzy, before they tumbled to the floor and she hiked her dress and positioned herself over him, his tumescent dick sliding easily into her familiar depths. She had been so happy to see his girlfriend get upset and leave. She had come prepared to seduce him and was not going to leave without fucking him. After tonight, he would be hers again.

Nicholas grunted something unintelligible. He felt like he was in another world. It had been so long since he'd been inside of her. He had forgotten how good it felt, how her plump, hairless pussy would drown his dick with its sweet, sticky juices. He groaned like a wounded animal as she increased her tempo, bouncing her way rapidly to an orgasm as her huge braless breasts threatened to pop out of the top of her dress.

"Nicky! Nicky! I'm coming! I'm coming baby! Oh yes!" she screamed as she climaxed all over his unsheathed dick, pounding his chest with her fists.

"Oh my God," she breathed, her eyes sparkling with triumph. She got up and went over to the sofa where she swung her right leg over the arm and bent over, her glistening flesh gaping, begging to be filled.

"Come and reclaim your pussy Nicky," she purred, looking back at him over her shoulder.

Nicholas got up with a growl and rushed over to her. He rammed his dick inside her.

"Yes! Fuck it Nicky! Fuck it hard Nicky! Take back your pussy Nicky!" she shouted fervently like an evangelist.

Nicholas didn't last long, the emotional abyss that he had been in since her call on Sunday swallowed him whole and he uttered a guttural roar as he climaxed, spilling his seed inside her.

He slid out of her and slumped to the floor, emotionally and physically spent.

He couldn't believe what had just happened. It seemed so surreal. Jesus Christ. How would he face Shari?

Chapter 8

Shari's alarm clock, which looked like a fat man's naked ass, a fun gift from one of her friends who lived in England, emitted a shrill cry at 6 a.m. She groaned and turned it off. She stared at the ceiling for about a minute, trying not to fall back asleep. She then reached over for her mobile. Three missed calls, but none from Nicholas. Shari got up and turned the radio on as she rummaged through the closet to select an outfit for work. The news was on.

A community is in mourning after gunmen invaded a home in the wee hours of the morning and killed four of the six people that were there, including two children, ages three and seven. The police surmise that the murders were committed because of an ongoing gang feud in the community.

Shari shook her head sadly as she placed the

navy blue skirt suit that she was going to wear on the bed. These criminals nowadays had no heart. Even the poor innocent kids weren't safe anymore. She went into the bathroom to brush her teeth when she came back into the bedroom abruptly. Something caught her ear on the news.

A man, identified as Nicholas Ramtalie, was killed in a motor vehicle accident on Washington Boulevard at approximately 1 a.m. when the driver of a newspaper delivery van, tired from working two shifts, fell asleep and crashed into Mr. Ramtalie's Mitsubishi Grandis killing him and injuring his unidentified female passenger, who was admitted to the hospital in serious but stable condition.

Shari leaned against the wall as she tried to wrap her brain around what she had just heard. Nicholas was dead? It had happened yet again. Another boyfriend was suddenly dead, under tragic circumstances. Sweet mother of Joseph. It had been happening since she was seventeen and now she was twenty-three and it was still occurring. She couldn't continue to go through this. As if in denial, she grabbed her phone and with trembling fingers, scrolled to Nicholas' mobile number and dialed it. It went straight to voice mail. Maybe someone had even stolen it from the scene of the accident.

Shari sat on the floor and cradled her head in her hands. What was Nicholas doing on Washington

Boulevard that hour of the morning? Dropping home that bitch of course. There was no question that she was the unidentified female passenger. Shari futilely brushed aside the tears. She hadn't loved him but she had cared about him. It was messed up that the last time she saw him she was upset with him. It also hurt a bit that he had taken that woman inside the house. They certainly hadn't stood outside and talked for hours; that's for sure.

There was no doubt that they had had a reunion fuck. Shari sighed. Why was she so unlucky with men? Why did her boyfriends keep on dying? She just couldn't understand it. It was as though she was cursed. Half an hour passed before she managed to get up from the floor and go inside the bathroom. She threw up a few times before crawling back into bed. There was no way she could function at work today. She needed at least a day to get herself together. She decided to call the boss and let him know that she wouldn't be coming in.

He sounded like he was at home having breakfast when she called. He was alarmed at the way she sounded but she told him not to worry, she would be fine and would be back at work tomorrow.

She hung up and pulled the covers over her head.

She cried until she fell asleep from sheer exhaustion.

Chapter 9

"C'mon Shari...you haven't been out in so long," Yanique beseeched. She and Justine were talking to Shari on three-way.

It had been a month since Nicholas' funeral and they were trying to convince Shari to go to a party with them. It promised to be the hottest all-inclusive party of the year so far and they wanted their girl there with them.

Shari sighed. She knew she had to shake off the doldrums and get back to being her outgoing and fun self. Dealing with the death of yet another boyfriend had not been easy. Valentine's Day had been three weeks ago and she had spent it alone, eating pistachio ice cream and watching a DVD of Michael Jordan's last NBA season as a member of the Chicago Bulls. Justine and Yanique had offered to spend the day with her but she had adamantly told them to go ahead on their dates as she would be fine.

Fortunately her work had not suffered, if anything, February had been one of the most profitable months the company had seen in a long time, prompting Mr. Morgan, her boss, to quip 'What recession?'. She had poured all of her time and energy into the job, using it as therapy. It had worked to some degree. Her accomplishments for the month had made her feel really good about herself. But she still had to sort out her personal life. She had taken an oath at Nicholas' funeral, as she watched the casket being lowered into the ground, that she would never get involved in another serious relationship. From now on, she would only have casual relationships. Fuck buddies and one night stands. No strings attached. She refused to go through this again but she still needed to have a life. This was her compromise. She wasn't used to that sort of lifestyle but sometimes one had to work with the cards they're dealt.

"Ok," she finally agreed. "I'll meet you guys there."

"Hell no," Yanique said. "We'll come by your house and we all go together in your ride."

Shari chuckled. They were afraid she would change her mind.

"Ok, whatever," she responded. "Well its just 9 O' clock so I'll see you guys around 12?"

"Yeah, we'll be there by 12," Yanique agreed.

Shari hung up and went into the bedroom. She pulled out a suitcase from the bottom of her closet. It contained several new pieces that she hadn't yet worn. She felt like going all out tonight. She selected a sexy red form fitting Donna Karan sweater dress and an exquisite pair of black Emillio Pucci pumps that she had splurged on the last time she went to New York a few months ago. Her black and red Michael Kors Marina Zip clutch purse would complete her ensemble. She smiled. Nothing like a blazing outfit to cheer a girl right on up. She was positive that she would be the hottest looking girl at the party.

CR...&)CR...&)

Karim arrived at the party at 1 p.m. Taj, his good friend and business partner, was with him as was Kimberly and two girls that Taj had brought with him, a Puerto Rican from Miami that he was seeing and her best friend, also a Latina. The girls were gorgeous. Kimberly, as good as she looked, was no match for the sheer beauty and exotic sex appeal of the two Latinas and it pissed her off to no end. Karim noticed the change in her attitude when they met up with the others in the parking lot but he didn't comment. He was in a very good mood and planned to enjoy himself. And if Kimberly wanted to be bitchy, he would just ignore her. They made their way through the crowd and headed straight to one of the four bars set up inside the venue.

"Lets chill out over there," Karim suggested, gesturing to a little spot close to the fence between the bar and the body painting booth.

Taj nodded and they made their way over there, with lots of eyes following the well dressed, attractive group. Karim surveyed the crowd coolly as he sipped his vodka and cranberry and rocked to the infectious beat of Lil Wayne's hit single *Mrs. Officer.* The party was in full swing and like any good party the women outnumbered the men at least three to one. Global recession or not, Jamaicans were going to party, and look good while doing it. He glanced at a group of three girls that had just walked over to the bar. His eyes met with the short one's and held. Shari. Damn she looked hot. She was wearing the hell out of that red dress. She turned away after giving him a quick wave. Karim sighed wistfully. It was the first time he was seeing her since he saw her on Super Bowl Sunday at the sports bar in New Kingston. And he was still having the same reaction. He wanted her.

Kimberly hugged him and whispered in his ear, cutting into his thoughts. He could smell the intoxicating scent of the Marc Jacobs perfume that he had bought her a few weeks ago.

"Why are you staring at that bitch like that?" she queried, softening her question by caressing his back.

Karim lit a cigarette and looked at her.

"Because she looks good," he replied, exhaling a cloud of smoke.

Kimberly frowned. She knew the girl. They had attended the same college but had moved in different circles.

"Don't be mean," she pouted.

Karim tuned her out mentally. Seeing Shari again was making him reassess his stance that he wasn't going to pursue her.

Kimberly then got in front of him and started dancing, grinding her ass against his pelvis to the sounds of Busy Signal's *Tic Tok*. The disc jockey had turned the beat around, intensifying the energy level of the crowd. A small triumphant smile played at the corners of her full lips when she felt his dick responding to her gyrations. She now had his full attention.

CR...SOCR...SO

Shari thought about Karim as she sipped her white wine. She was surprised to see him. He looked even better than she remembered. He looked really trendy in his black and white striped cardigan, white shirt and skinny black tie dressed down with fitted jeans and black patent leather high-top air force ones. Best dressed guy in the party hands down. She wondered if that uptown bimbo was his girlfriend. If that was the case he could do much better. She looked nice enough but she was a bitch. A non-ambitious airhead who thought she was the shit. Used to walk around campus with her nose in the air like she was better than everybody else. But what did she care. Maybe those were the kind of girls he went for. Pretty and brainless. Surface level bitches who thought that looking hot was all there was to life.

She laughed as Yanique did her signature move, bending slightly and shaking her voluptuous ass mightily to the sounds of her favourite get wild song, Beenie Man's *Back it Up* while Justine dramatically pretended to smack it. She loved her crazy friends. She didn't know what she would do without them.

CR...ƧƆCR...ƧƆ

Karim looked at the ceiling fan spinning slowly as he smoked a cigarette. Kimberly's red thong was still on it. He had thrown it in the air behind him when he had ripped her clothes off when they arrived at his apartment after the party. After seven drinks and Kimberly gyrating on him most of the night, he was horny as hell by the time he got home. The sex had been great, as usual, but that was all there was to it. He glanced over at Kimberly's sleeping form. He really needed to cut her loose. Their relationship, if you could call it that, was going nowhere and she was taking up too much of his physical and emotional space, wanting to be around him constantly and calling him all the time like he was her man. He went to great pains to explain to her that they weren't exclusive or anything like that and that she was free to see other people but she still liked to act like they were a couple. He thought about Shari for the umpteenth time that night as he stubbed his cigarette in the ashtray. He really, really liked her. And he was going to let her know that real soon. He rolled over and pulled the comforter up to his neck. He was soon fast asleep.

Chapter 10

Shari woke up at 11:40 a.m. the following morning. The first thing she realized, even with her stomach growling in an unfeminine manner indicating that it was empty, was that she was still horny. It had taken her forever to fall asleep when she got in at 4 this morning. The four glasses of white wine had seemed to head straight between her legs. She was soaking wet by the time she got home. It had taken a quickie with Tickler, her vibrator, to ease the ache and allow her to fall asleep. She blushed as she remembered that she had thought about Karim the entire time she was pleasuring herself.

She still couldn't understand why she was so attracted to him. As hot as he was, and he was smoking hot, he wasn't the kind of guy she usually went for. She needed to stay as far away from him as possible. If she was so attracted to him and she barely knew him that meant big trouble. She absolutely was not going down that road. Shari got up and went into the bathroom. She peed and then took a quick shower. She planned to swing by the Flamingo Hotel for Sunday brunch. A lot of rich older men were always there. Maybe one of them would get lucky today.

Today was as good a day as any to try out her new approach to sex and relationships.

CR...SOCR...SO

"But I wanted to spend the day with you," Kimberly whined as they left his apartment. Karim opened the car door and got in. This girl was seriously getting on his last nerve.

"Kimberly, what the fuck is your problem?" he asked as he gunned the engine. "How many times do I have to tell you that we're not a couple?"

"But we've gotten closer since you first said that Karim...what's the problem? You don't think I'm good enough for you? Do you know who my father is? I come from a very prominent family. Do you have any idea how many men want me?" Kimberly seethed, not used to not getting what she wanted.

Karim chuckled mirthlessly. "No but they can all have you."

Kimberly sulked in silence for the entire twenty minute drive to where she lived in the family home in Jacks Hill. She got out and slammed his car door shut without saying goodbye. Karim glared at her retreating back as she strode angrily up the cobblestone driveway. He hated when anyone slammed his car door. *Good fucking riddance,* he mused as he reversed and turned the car around, though he knew deep down that Kimberly would not give up that easily. His mobile rang as he headed down the hill. It was the guy who wanted to buy his car. He was planning to sell it as he figured it was time to upgrade to an SUV. He loved the coupe. He had bought it brand new a year and a half ago and it was still a beauty but the guy was willing to pay top dollar for it so what the hell. And, truth be told, the fact that Shari drove an SUV had something to do with him wanting to change his vehicle soon. He didn't think that she was that shallow but something told him that she didn't like cars and what a man drove was an extension of his personality for the most part. He had to come correct.

CR...SOCR...SO

"Mmmm...oh yeah...just like that..." Mrs. Dell-Fisher, Yanique's boss, moaned as she ran her hands through Yanique's extensions. "God I love your tongue ...lick it baby...oh yeah...lick this pussy dry..."

Yanique stuck her tongue inside Mrs. Dell-Fisher's pussy as far as it would go and wiggled it like it was possessed.

"Oh fuck! I'm coming!" Mrs. Dell-Fisher declared breathlessly as her petite body stiffened in anticipation of her impending orgasm. It would be her third of the afternoon. She couldn't wait for Yanique to put on the ten inch strap-on and fuck her senseless. But she was getting ahead of herself.

One orgasm at a time.

"Ahhhhh! Fucking hell!" she squealed as waves of pleasure rippled through her frame.

"But what the fuck is this I'm seeing?" a deep voice bellowed rhetorically from the open bedroom door.

Mrs. Dell-Fisher tumbled down from her orgasmic cloud. Merrick? What the hell was he doing home so early? He should be at the Roxbury Club playing squash right now.

Yanique jerked upright and turned around, her mouth slick with Mrs. Dell-Fisher's juices.

"Merrick!" Mrs. Dell-Fisher exclaimed. How was she going to explain this? "I-"

"I what?" her husband thundered, stopping her in mid-sentence as he strode over to the bed angrily. Yanique jumped off the bed and hastily grabbed her clothes. She needed to get the hell out of there. She came over here to fuck, not to get caught up in any drama. "I was just having an afternoon snack? Is that what you were going to say? Huh? You fuck-ing slut!"

He grabbed his wife and hauled her off the bed unceremoniously. He shook her like a rag doll and slapped her face, his massive hand leaving its imprint on her right jaw.

"Oh God! Please Merrick! Let me explain!" she cried as she tried to stop the blows. Her attempts were futile. She hollered as he threw her back down on the bed and slapped her repeatedly.

Yanique was horrified. She wanted to help Mrs. Dell-Fisher but the best thing to do was to make a quick exit. After all, she was in the man's home having sex with his wife in their marital bed. Eschewing her underwear, she hurriedly pulled on her jeans and grabbed her top, pulling it on as she made her way to the door.

"You! Where do think you're going?" Merrick Fisher shouted as he hopped off the bed and tackled Yanique. She fell to the floor with a thud. She kicked her feet out and one caught him in the face. Enraged, he stumbled to his feet and grabbed a fist-ful of her braids and punched her viciously in her right side.

"Bloodclaat!" Yanique blurted in pain, shocked that he would attack her. The man was crazy. She swung her elbow and caught him dead on the chin.

He staggered back and she dashed through the door with him hot on her heels.

"Come back here you big dyke bitch!" he shouted, as he caught up with her in the expansive living room after she bumped her thigh against a table. Adrenaline pumping, Yanique wrestled with the man, giving as good as she got. He punched her in the left eye and she bit him on the neck, drawing blood. He screamed as she followed that up with a kick to his testicles. He doubled over in pain and she ran outside, still in shock at what had just transpired.

The gardener, leaning on his rake and laughing until tears ran down his face, watched as Yanique jumped in her car and sped off in a daze, her eye throbbing painfully. It had been fun, exploring her bi-curious side with her boss, and enjoying certain perks at work, but it had unexpectedly and dramatically blown up in her face big time.

What the hell was going to happen now?

CR...SOCR...SO

Shari smiled at the man's lame joke. She was in the middle of her scrumptious brunch: fried shrimp in batter with a sweet chili dip and a smoked marlin and pasta salad. She had missed breakfast as they stopped serving that at 11, but she didn't mind, the lunch buffet was fabulous. The man, who had asked her if he could join her five minutes into her meal, was a partner at Blake, Richards and Young, a law firm that specialized in litigation, considered himself to have a great sense of humor. Shari was clueless as to how he arrived at that conclusion. But that didn't matter. He was relatively attractive, clean cut, married and over forty. Perfect for a no strings attached afternoon romp. He didn't know her and hopefully, they would never see each other again. She daintily chewed her food as he prattled on, trying to impress her.

"What are you doing after lunch?" Shari queried, tired of his banal banter.

"I pretty much have the afternoon free," he responded, a bemused expression on his face. "Why?"

"Would you like to feed on my pussy after lunch... or will you be too full?" Shari asked, her innocent expression belying her wanton question.

Richards choked on his seafood lasagna.

Shari smiled sweetly and sipped her pineapple juice. It was a liberating feeling, this new approach. She felt powerful and very new age if you will. She watched as he composed himself.

"I would very much like that," he finally said, wiping his mouth with his napkin. His whole body language had changed. He was now charged with excitement. Shari was sure that the entire hotel could operate on the energy radiating from his body right about now.

"Good," Shari responded as she placed a spoonful of the pasta in her mouth.

Richards was unable to finish his meal.

He was too excited.

Today must be his birthday.

Chapter 11

They went to a hotel all the way up in Smokey Vale, a hilly area several miles outside of Kingston. The view was great but Shari didn't think that was enough to justify the ridiculous real estate prices of the area. Richards paid for the room using his credit card, and Shari, feeling a bit nervous with her cute face partially hidden by her oversized Chanel aviator sunglasses, strutted behind him as he led the way to the room.

He opened the door and stepped aside for her to enter. She did and went straight into the bathroom to freshen up. She emerged from the bathroom a few minutes later and found Richards reclining on the bed. He was still fully dressed.

Shari took a deep breath and placed her pocketbook and shades on the dresser. This wasn't going to be as easy as she thought. Her insides were churning. Could she really do this? Fuck a man she just met? Only one way to find out. She walked over to him, her steady gait a stark contrast to her insides, which felt like jelly. Richards watched her with lust filled eyes. It was obvious that he was hard. The front of his Polo khaki shorts was inflated. Shari reached down and caressed it. It felt like a brick. Good. She could feel the nervousness giving way to the need to have the itch between her legs scratched by a hard dick.

"Mmmm...I'm so hard it hurts," Richards murmured, taking off his brown Polo shirt. It was obvious that he worked out. He was in pretty good shape.

Shari purred in approval. Her experiment was off to a good start. He got up and removed his shorts and underwear. Shari started undressing. He helped her. He stooped down and pulled down her denim skirt.

She could hear the sharp intake of his breath as he admired her body from his vantage point. Shari unhooked her bra and threw it on the bed. She looked down as he slowly removed her pink Victoria Secret thong.

"Damn you're sexy," he breathed before kissing her pussy gently.

"Mmmm," Shari moaned. "Get on the bed."

Richards did her bidding.

Shari got over him and lowered her pussy onto his open mouth. Open in shock from her take-charge attitude as well as in anticipation of tasting her smooth fleshy fruit.

"Yeah...mmmm...oh yeah...suck my sweet pussy...get it nice and wet..." she instructed as he licked and sucked her noisily, enjoying the feel of her fleshy folds against his tongue and lips.

Shari fucked his face until she felt her climax surging to her center.

"Fuck yeah! I'm about to come all over your fucking face! Drink up! Drink all of this sweet love juice!" she growled. "Ahhhhh! Ahhhhh! Yes Lord!"

Richards continued sucking her hungrily as she climaxed, intensifying her orgasm.

"Oh God! That was a nice appetizer," she breathed as she collapsed on the bed and reclined on the pillows.

She spread her legs wantonly, now thoroughly immersing herself in the moment. Gone were her inhibitions about fucking a total stranger. She was enjoying herself so far and now she was ready for the main event.

Her clit was throbbing unbearably.

She wanted some dick.

Now.

"I'm ready for the main event. Stop drooling and start fucking," Shari told him as she slipped a finger inside her wetness. Richards almost climaxed when she brought the finger to her lips and licked it clean. He hurriedly rolled on a condom and climbed on top of her. Shari spread her legs as wide as possible and he plunged inside her, grunting like a wild boar.

"Yes! Fuck me! Give me all you got!" Shari urged, slapping him on the ass.

"Argghgh! Jesus Christ!" Richards blurted as he climaxed with his fourth stroke.

Shari's mouth was a wide O as she watched him shake like a tsunami.

"You've got to be kidding me! What the fuck?" Shari said as she pushed him off of her. "You better get that shit back up!"

Richards' brown, oval face reddened in embarrassment.

"Just calm down...I don't know what happened... guess I was a bit too anxious but just give me a few minutes," he implored.

Sahri looked at him darkly through narrowed eyes.

"You've got fifteen minutes," she told him disgusted-ly. She had heard about one minute men but this was ridiculous. He hadn't even lasted a minute. If she wasn't so frustrated this shit would have been funny.

But this was no laughing matter.

Maybe later, but not right now.

She looked at her watch for emphasis.

She wasn't playing.

Her pussy throbbed impatiently.

CR...ಐ)CR...ಐ)

After meeting up with the young man who was interested in purchasing his car, Karim went up to Armour Heights where Taj stayed when he was in Jamaica. It was a huge family house where only his mother and younger sister lived. He was out by the poolside with the two Latinas when Karim arrived.

"What's poppin'?" Taj greeted from his perch on a lounge chair where he was drinking Hypnotiq and red bull. A lit marijuana joint resting on an ashtray permeated the cool air with its intoxicating scent. A Mac rested on his lap. A design that he was working on was on the colourful screen.

The two Latinas were sitting on the edge of the pool with their feet dangling in the water. Their wet bronzed skins glistened in the brilliant Sunday afternoon sunshine. The one Taj was seeing was wearing a colourful Cavalli two-piece while the other had on a barely there green and white striped Juicy Couture set.

"Hi *Papi*," they said in unison, flashing gorgeous smiles.

"Hello ladies," Karim responded, his gaze lingering on the two exotic women.

"She likes you," Taj said to Karim as he sat down on the chair beside him and reached into the ice bucket to fix himself a drink. "Alondra told me last night that Olivia thought you were *muy caliente.*"

Karim chuckled. "How long are they staying?"

"They'll be here with me until Thursday," Taj replied, taking a strong toke of the marijuana joint. "They're off the chain...I wanted to have a threesome with them this morning but even though she fucked Alondra with me in the room, she wouldn't allow me to touch her. Said she was saving it for you."

Karim chuckled again and looked at Olivia. She was a beautiful girl. Resembled Eva Mendez but had a body like Jennifer Lopez, with the booty to match. He could feel a stirring in his loins. Latin women had that fire. He was sure she would be fantastic in bed. As if reading his thoughts, she returned his gaze and playfully licked her lips before smiling and going into the water. He watched her swim to the deep end of the pool, slicing through the water gracefully like a sexy mermaid.

"Sounds good to me," Karim said, sipping his drink. "Really good..."

Taj laughed.

They then discussed business for the next half an hour until the girls exited the pool. Olivia stood in full view of Karim and dried herself with a large, fluffy Hello Kitty towel. She then gave him the look, captivating him with her gorgeous brown-green eyes and walked slowly inside. Karim's eyes rolled hypnotically from side to side with each sensuous sway of her wide hips.

He refilled his drink and followed.

CR...℘CR...℘

"What the fuck happened to your face?" Shari asked Yanique the moment she entered the house. She had been on her way home from her disappointing afternoon rendezvous when Yanique had called, asking her to swing by.

Yanique sat on the couch and smiled at Shari as she touched the left side of her face gingerly. It was swollen and hurt like hell. Her eye was also black and blue.

She was halfway into telling a wide-eyed Shari what had happened when Justine walked in.

"Bumboclaat!" she exclaimed when she saw Yanique's face. "What happened to you?"

She had to start the story over.

When she was through all three of them burst out laughing. It was scary and the man needed to pay for what he did to her but the incident was also hilarious.

"I can't believe this," Shari said when their laughter subsided. "That man is fucking insane. You need to go to the police. I mean, look at your face."

Yanique shook her head. "Nah, no cops. But I plan to get him back though. I'm taking this one to the streets. Remember my cousin Double Ugly from Spanish Town? He just got out of prison for wounding with intent last week. He's coming to see me later. He will deal with it."

Shari sighed. So much drama. First her frustrating foray into the realm of casual sex and now Yanique had been in a fight with her boss' husband after he caught them in bed together.

"I think you need to go to the doctor," Shari said, going up close and looking at Yanique's face critically. "You might need antibiotics and stuff."

Yanique nodded in agreement.

"I plan to, I just had to calm down and cool off first. There's a doctor on Hagley Park road that's open on a Sunday until 7."

"Well we'll go with you," Shari said, looking at Justine for confirmation.

"Of course," Justine agreed though she had planned to go to the movies with Terrence, the guy she was currently dating. She would just have to call and cancel. They could go and see Tyler Perry's new movie another time.

"I could have beaten him up if we weren't at his house," Yanique bragged, wincing as she laughed. Any kind of facial movement was painful. Even blinking.

Shari laughed. It was entirely possible. Yanique was a big girl and she was aggressive. Shari didn't doubt that the man had received a few good blows as well.

"So what is going to happen now?" Shari asked. "I mean...she's your boss..."

"Well I don't know yet...I'm going to get the doctor to give me the rest of the week off from work to recuperate," Yanique replied. "I'll see what happens when I go back to work next week."

"If he did you like *that* I can only imagine what he did to his wife," Justine mused, adding, "and can you imagine if it was a man he had caught screwing his wife? He would have killed them both!"

Yanique chuckled wryly. "She's small like Shari; poor thing might be in the hospital right now."

"I'm not small...I'm fun-sized," Shari retorted. "And as big and strong as Yanique is he probably thought it was a man fucking his wife."

They all laughed, especially Justine, who tumbled to the floor, laughing until she needed a glass of water.

CR...SOCR...SO

Karim, knowing the house well, headed straight to the guest room that was next to Taj's room on the right side of the house which was away from the section where his mother and sister stayed. Olivia was standing in front of the full length mirror removing her clothes when he entered the room and shut the door behind him. He watched her watch him through the mirror as she undressed. God she was sexy. The total physical package: beauty, ass and breasts with the kind of dimensions that were a visual paradise. A woman that could seduce any man effortlessly.

He sipped his drink and walked over to her, pulling her roughly to him. She looked at him, her luscious pink lips quivering, her eyes speaking to him in the universal language. Sex. He kissed her deeply. She moaned in his mouth as she returned his kiss passionately, kissing him like she had done so a thousand times before, her sweet, nimble tongue playing around in his mouth with sensuous familiarity.

"I wanted you from the first time I laid eyes on you *papacito*," she confessed, her sexy accent sending chills up his spine then down his groin.

She broke the kiss and took a sip of his drink before sliding down slowly until she was squatting in front of him. She pulled the zipper on his grey Rock Republic jeans and freed his rock-hard dick.

"*Tu pene es muy grande*," she breathed as ran her tongue along the length of his shaft, her mesmerizing brown-green eyes looking up at him seductively.

Karim groaned like a wounded animal.

He ran his hands through her flowing mane. It was soft and silky.

She then took him in her mouth, working her way down his shaft, sucking in more and more of him like a hoover until she swallowed it all. She impressively held all eight inches of him for several seconds before she came up gasping for air. She massaged his testicles as she looked up at him, her eyes gleaming with lust as she caught her breath.

"Mmmm...*Papacito...te necesito* to fuck me," Olivia breathed, her sultry accent and wanton words making Karim harder than a sack of bricks. He swelled even more in her soft hands. He couldn't recall ever being this hard in his entire life.

She rose and lifted his shirt over his head and quickly removed his white wife beater. She moaned in approval as she caressed his broad chest and sucked his nipples. Karim couldn't take it anymore. He tore off his jeans and boxers and quickly rolled on a lubricated condom.

He bent her over the dresser and entered her dripping orifice with a firm thrust.

"Ohhh...fucking *animale salvaje...papacito...* it hurts...hurts good....*bueno*...ooohhh..." she moaned as they maintained eye contact through the mirror.

She had the most beautiful fuck face that Karim had ever seen. Even with her face contorted in ecstasy she looked gorgeous. Karim stroked her slowly but firmly, going deep inside her succulent heat. She was tight. Her sugar walls squeezed his dick as it plunged in and out, seemingly increasing its pace with each stroke.

"*Si papi! Si! Carajo! Carajo! Dios mios! Dios mios! Estoy por acabar!*" she screamed as she climaxed, her body shaking like an exquisite over-sized vibrator. She was shaking so hard that Karim stopped moving, his dick still embedded deep inside her, and just watched in amazement as she came and came and came. He had never seen anything like it.

He resumed stroking her, gripping her wide hips tightly and plunging in hard and deep. Her pussy was so good it felt like he didn't even have on a condom. This girl was dangerous.

"*Yo quiero su dedo en mi culo!*" she shouted, her face a mask of passionate disbelief. She was getting ready to come again and she couldn't believe it. Realizing that Karim didn't understand what she just said, she told him again, this time in English.

"I want your finger in my ass," she told him, her full, firm breasts jiggling mightily with each violent thrust.

Karim stuck his right thumb in her mouth for lubrication before slipping it inside her anus as he continued to fuck her at a torrid pace.

"Ohhhh! *Dios Mios! Dios Mios!*" she shrieked as she climaxed yet again, sweeping her hand across the dresser in an orgasmic frenzy, sending perfume bottles and a vase with orchids onto the carpeted floor.

Karim pulled out of her and she slumped to the floor. Her chest heaved mightily as she tried to catch her breath.

"*Papacito*...you're the fucking best...splash your *leche* all over my face..." she implored.

Karim had no doubt about what she meant this time. He ripped off the condom and she scrambled to her knees as he positioned his dick in front of her face.

She licked his testicles as he pumped his throbbing dick furiously.

"Give it to me *papi*...mmmm...now *papi*...now... empty your *cojones*," she urged, her brown-green eyes shining lustfully.

"Mmmm...mmmm...mmmm..." she moaned, licking what she could as he showered her face with his juices. *"Dulce como la miel."*

He tumbled onto the floor next to her. He felt deliciously drained. There was something about coming all over a beautiful woman's face that drove him wild. He looked at her in wonder. She was in no rush to clean his unborn children from off her face.

"Sweet like honey," she whispered, her brown-green eyes twinkling in delight.

Karim laughed heartily.

Olivia was a gorgeous, sexy freak.

The kind of woman a man could get addicted to quite easily.

He sighed.

If things didn't work out when he pursued Shari, Olivia could possibly be the one.

After all, it was unwise to put all your eggs in one basket.

hapter 12

Shari was not in the best of moods. She was now home after dropping off Justine and Yanique.

Yanique had gotten antibiotics, painkillers and a cream to rub on the wound; and the doctor had indeed given her a week off from work.

She was still horny and now, angry as well. Richards had turned out to be a dud. Even after he had managed to get hard again after feasting on her pussy and tossing her salad for over twenty minutes, he still could only better his previous record by two strokes. One. Two. Three. Four. Five. Six. Then nothing but grunts and laboured breathing like he had actually just done something.

The oral had been good but shit, she needed to be fucked. She was peeved that she had given this stranger the privilege of having her body and he didn't even have the decency to please her. She had told him some choice words after the second debacle and the ride back to Kingston to pick up her SUV where she had left it in the hotel parking lot had been a silent, tension-filled one.

Shari sighed. Undeserving prick. Maybe what happened was a sign that she should not go down that road. Maybe casual sex was not for her. Then what was she supposed to do? Start dating someone and have them die on her once the relationship got serious? Nope. That was not an option, she told herself firmly, remembering the four painful times she'd had to endure it. She needed sex from to time to time. She couldn't have a man of her own. There was nothing else she could do. It had to be this way. She fervently hoped that the next person she chose to give a sample of her goodies would give a good account of himself.

CR...ᔓᕲCR...ᔓ

The following Wednesday, Karim, Taj, Alondra and Olivia went to a car dealership on Constant Spring Road that was owned by a friend of Karim's. Though he himself was part owner of a car dealership, they didn't sell SUVs so he had to get one elsewhere. He had called his friend to get an idea of the different SUVs he had in stock. He wanted to purchase something today so that he would have something to drive for the coming weekend. The guy he had sold his car to would be picking it up on Friday. His friend had a wide variety: X5s, Tundras, Pajeros, Montero Sports, Tacomas and a 2007 Dodge Ram.

His friend was unable to keep his eyes off the two women the entire time he was talking to Karim. He probably had daughters their ages but that didn't stop him from salivating like a horny schoolboy. Karim had met him when he had joined the Jamaica Motor Vehicle Association two years ago, and despite the vast age difference, they had become good friends.

After Karim chatted with him for a few minutes in his office, they then made their way out to the lot and went over to the section designated for trucks and SUVs.

After an hour of careful inspection, it came down to a choice between a white 2008 Toyota Tundra and the black 2007 Dodge Ram. The Ram was huge, had a quad cab and was tricked out with a DVD player, six disc CD changer, navigation system and red leather seats. It was in excellent condition and had never been driven on Jamaican roads. His friend said he could have it for 3 million. Karim knew that if he gave him 2.8 million, which he planned to do, he would take it.

The Tundra was also luxurious and hot and it had also never been driven in Jamaica. It was only a year old.

"So what you guys think?" Karim asked, though he had already chosen the Dodge Ram mentally.

"I like the big black one *papi*," Olivia opined in a sultry tone. Everyone grinned at her double entendre.

"Yeah, the Ram seems like the best choice," Taj agreed.

Alondra was the only one who thought he should take the Tundra, but that was because white was her favourite colour.

Karim then went back inside to speak to his friend while they waited for him in the reception area, watching the small TV mounted on the wall which was showing a live cricket match between England and the West Indies. Karim was back in fifteen minutes and the group of four made their way outside to Taj's metallic blue illegally fast Mitsubishi Evolution IX. Taj and the girls had come by his office to scoop him up. The girls were hungry so they decided to go to Dutch Pot, an authentic Jamaican restaurant on Holborn Road for lunch.

Karim didn't plan on spending more than another hour and a half with them as he had a 2:30 meeting at the office. He played with Olivia's right nipple through her pink Juicy Couture baby T. She smiled as her nipple hardened in immediate response to his delicate touch. They had been fucking like rabbits since Sunday. Tonight was her last night on the island and she told him that she wanted to sleep with him at his apartment. He had readily agreed.

She told him the other day that he was tempting her to stay in Jamaica. If he didn't want Shari so badly he would probably have invited Olivia to stay a while longer. Spend some quality time with her and get to know her better. She was a commercial model and part time nursing student. She had shown him some of her ad campaigns and advertisements on the internet. She was doing something with herself and he liked that.

With her looks, she could easily sit around looking pretty and allow a rich man to take care of her. She was seeing someone back in Miami but she said it wasn't anything too serious. She was really feeling him. The other night at the movies when the four of them had gone to see the action thriller *Taken*, she had whispered e*stoy enamorada* in his ear. She wouldn't tell him what it meant though. He had to ask Alondra, who had seemed very surprised that her friend had said that to him. I'm in love. Latin women loved hard and fast. He had heard that line in a movie once. Apparently there was some truth to it.

He glanced at her smooth legs, spilling tantalizingly from under her short denim skirt.

Oh yeah, if Shari didn't want to get with him, Olivia was definitely a keeper.

ℭ…ℬℭ…ℬ

Yanique's cousin from Spanish Town, Double Ugly, finally paid her a visit on Wednesday evening. He was a superstitious career criminal and despite the fact that his instincts have never helped to keep him out of jail, he always followed them nevertheless. He had a dream on Saturday night that he interpreted as a warning not to leave Spanish Town for the next three days so even though his cousin had told him that she had been beaten up by a man and he had promised to go and see her that evening, he knew that he wouldn't have gone to Kingston before today.

He parked the decrepit Toyota Corolla that he had borrowed from one of his cronies in front of Yanique's gate and entered the yard. He ignored the yapping of the dog belonging to the people who lived on the other side of the house and walked up to Yanique's verandah. The dog wisely kept its distance as it continued it's shrilly barking. He banged on the grill loudly.

"Who is it?" Yanique bellowed from inside the living room.

"Ah me cuz," he replied.

She came out and opened the grill, letting him in. His body odour almost made her retch. He smelled like he hadn't showered in days.

"What's up Double?" she said, stopping her breath as she gave him a quick hug.

He didn't mind his name as he had had it since he was three years old. He had a face that not even a mother could love. His face looked like a cruel joke, as though it was constructed by someone who just haphazardly put it together without seeing the need for coordination and symmetry. His huge nose seemed to be too close to his sunken eyes and his small fish-like mouth was filled with teeth so huge that most of them remained outside, seemingly unable to properly fit inside his mouth.

"Nothing much," he said, stepping inside the house. "What you have to drink?"

"Would you like a Guiness?" she asked, heading into the kitchen.

"Yeah man, a hot one," he replied.

She bought it to him and sat as far away from him as possible, perching on the sofa closest to the door.

He sipped the Guiness thirstily, belching loudly after he finally removed the bottle from his mouth, half its contents gone.

He looked at her face, which though still a mess, was looking much better than it did three days ago.

The eye was still black and blue but the swelling had gone down considerably and she could now wash her face without whimpering in pain.

"Tell me what happen," he said.

She did and he listened, his sunken coal-black eyes blazing with anger. But she misconstrued what he was angry about.

He flew off the sofa and grabbed his startled cousin, and brought her face close to his.

"Yuh did ah fuck de man wife?" he growled rhetorically. "Yuh is a sodomite! De man should 'ave kill yuh rass!"

He pushed her back onto the sofa and slapped her viciously in the face.

Yanique was too shocked to speak. She couldn't believe he was reacting like this. She held her jaw as her eyes watered. Double Ugly had massive hands. Getting slapped by him was like being hit by a paddle.

"If yuh wasn't mi cousin, mi would pump two shot into yuh nasty bloodclaat right now!" he shouted, spittle flying like miniature missiles from his rancid mouth.

Yanique thought it best not to speak. Why was he so angry? Even if he didn't condone that kind of lifestyle her revelation shouldn't have prompted such a violent reaction. He was so angry he was shaking. He looked like he was going to hit her again.

"Double! The man has money! Just take the address and you can go over there and rob him! Don't you need money?" she said quickly, knowing that would distract him. "Trust me...a whole heap of money supposed to be inside the house."

"Gimme de address," he growled roughly, eager to get away from her before he lost control.

She got up to write it down then remembering that he couldn't read too well, verbally gave him directions to the Fishers' home. He left abruptly and she quickly closed the grill and door. She cried as she went into the bathroom to look at her face. The imprint of his big, dirty fingers was on her right jaw.

That definitely did not go as planned. Something must be mentally wrong with her cousin. Why did he do that to her? She was one of the few family members that he had who at least kept in touch with him and helped him out every now and then. And this was the thanks she got.

Instead of being upset that the man had beaten up his cousin, sending her to the doctor with injuries, he was upset that she had been fucking the man's wife. If she hadn't told him that he could get money from the man's house he would have probably beaten her up and left without defending her honour.

Well this was it.

From now on she would deal with him like most of the family did.

Pretend he didn't exist.

Chapter 13

Double Ugly dragged on his cigarette harshly as he made his way to Barbican, where the man lived. He was upset at himself for dealing with his cousin so roughly but what she had told him had forced him to reluctantly confront his own demons. He had had sex with several men during his last trip to prison. He was still trying to convince himself that he was not gay, that it was the long stretch he did that had gotten to him. Prior to doing those four and a half years, he had been to jail and prison many times but had never been incarcerated for longer than a year.

He failed miserably at his efforts. Every time he heard a song, or heard someone make reference to anything homosexual, he felt an unbridled rage and utter disgust with himself. If the men in his community found out about his actions while in prison, they would kill him. He had had sex with one of the girls from the community – she only agreed because she was deathly afraid of him – the same day he had been released from prison and during the act, while fucking her doggystyle, he had pulled out and forcefully entered her anus, using his big paws to silence her screams. He had threatened to kill her if she told anyone. The girl had left the community the following morning. She went back to the country to stay with her grandmother.

He shrugged aside his thoughts and focused on the matter at hand as he pulled up in front of the house. He parked slightly beyond the gate and got out. The electronic gate was open but was closing slowly; apparently someone had just driven in. Throwing caution to the wind, he pulled out his firearm and slipped inside. A man was taking some things from off the backseat of a white Toyota Prado. He rushed up to him and held the gun to his head.

"Pussy! Don't make a sound," he snarled, his fetid breath making the man heave.

"Don't kill me, just take whatever you want," the man babbled nervously.

Double Ugly smashed the 357 magnum hard against the man's skull, opening up a wound on the right side of his balding head.

"You have a hearing problem...mi nuh just blood-claat tell yuh say yuh nuffi make a sound," he growled, pulling the man away from the car and walking with him towards the front door.

"Anybody else deh home?" Double Ugly asked, his eyes scanning around furtively to see if he spotted anyone observing them.

The man nodded. "My wife is home and the helper might still be here."

"Open de door and go inside," Double Ugly instructed, pressing the cold metal against the back of the man's head.

They entered the house and Double Ugly used his right foot to shut the door.

The house was quiet.

"Call out to yuh wife," he told the man.

"Marilyn? Marilyn!" he called out, his voice cracking with fear. He was a big, strong man, but the man behind him was just as big, had a gun to his head and was clearly not a novice at this. Struggling with him was out of the question. His licensed firearm was outside in his vehicle anyway.

"Maybe she's sleeping," he said to his tormentor.

Double Ugly nudged him forward. "Go to the bedroom."

He had a throaty quality to his voice that disturbed his victim. *Oh God, he's going to rape my wife!*

The thought of another man penetrating his wife was almost too much to bear. He was extremely jealous and possessive of his wife of twelve years. Ten years his junior, she was like fine wine, getting better with each passing year. At thirty-nine, she still looked like she was in her mid-twenties. He had been sorry for the brutal beating he had given her after catching her in bed with that dyke bitch but he couldn't have helped himself.

She had deserved it. She had defiled their home. Turned their bedroom into Sodom and Gomorrah. He led the way to the bedroom and opened the door. His wife, wearing one of his T-shirts, was on the bed sleeping. She was covered up to the waist. His leather bound copy of the King James Version of the bible lay on the bed beside her.

"Where is de money?" Double Ugly asked him in a gruff whisper.

He pointed to the closet.

"Go for it...an' trust mi...nuh try fi be a hero," Double Ugly told him, smashing him in the head with the gun once more for emphasis.

Blood flowed freely.

"Oww!" he squealed, holding his head and feeling the fresh flow of warm blood. It was a nasty gash, worse than the first one based on the amount of blood flowing.

Double Ugly stayed close to him as he pushed his suits to one side and slid open a compartment in the back of the closet. In it were stacks of money in different currencies and a jewellery box.

Double Ugly smiled.

He instructed the man to put everything inside the black carry-on that was on the floor to the right of the large closet.

He took the carry-on from the man and placed it by the bedroom door. He then instructed him to use two of his neckties to tie up his wife.

She woke up with a start when he started to bind her hands.

"Ssshhhh!" he whispered, sweat from his frightened face dripping on her equally frightened face along with the blood leaking from the two wounds on his head.

She looked beyond him and saw the intruder holding the gun. She gasped loudly but thankfully managed not to scream. Who knows what he would have done had the scream not died in her throat.

He was without a doubt the ugliest living creature she had ever laid eyes upon. And he was here in her bedroom, with her and her husband at his mercy. Oh God. What had she done to deserve all the bad things that had happened to her this week? First her husband had caught her in bed with Yanique and beat her to a pulp, incredibly not breaking any of her bones, and now this: something from the depths of hell in their home, and God knows what he would do to them before making his escape.

She wondered if Beulah, the helper, had already gone home. She hoped so. Because if he was in here with them that meant he had probably killed her. She watched the man with terrified eyes as she meekly allowed her husband to tie her hands and legs. The man had a predatory look in his sunken, impossibly black eyes. He was going to rape her. She felt sick. If he touched her she was sure she would die from choking on her own vomit.

She watched in wide-eyed shock as the man told her husband to drop his pants.

Her husband nearly fainted. His eyes bulged and his mouth opened unnaturally, like he was slack jawed. He turned his head to look at his captor and received a crushing blow to his face, breaking his nose. He released a piercing scream which was cut short by the gun being shoved roughly into his mouth, breaking several of his teeth on entry.

"Mi say to drop yuh bumboclaat pants and yuh boxers or panty...whichever one yuh wear. Mi neva tell yuh to look on mi!" the man growled before slowly removing the gun and resuming his position behind him.

Marilyn Dell-Fisher could not believe her eyes. The man was a homosexual. He was going to violate her husband right before her very eyes. She could feel the bile rising in her throat.

Gasping in pain, shock and incredulity, her husband moved in slow motion as he unbuckled his pants and let them fall to his ankles. His blue cotton briefs followed.

He cried silent tears as he heard the man pull his zipper.

He wet himself as the man, using the gun, nudged him to bend over.

"Police! Freeze! Don't fucking move!" came a shout from the bedroom doorway.

Chapter 14

Double Ugly, startled, turned around and when the cops saw the weapon in his hand they let loose, making his body do a comical dance routine as they peppered him with bullets. His dead, bullet-riddled body fell to the carpeted floor with a dull thud. Mr. Fisher sustained a bullet wound in the ass. The police, snickering at the bizarre scene that had greeted them, rushed him to a private hospital along with his wife who was suffering from severe trauma.

Fortunately for Fisher, he had only been grazed on the buttocks by the bullet. The offending ass cheek was bandaged as were the two head wounds. His broken nose fortunately did not require surgery and was popped back in place. The doctor prescribed him some medication and he was sent home three hours after arriving at the hospital. Mrs. Dell-Fisher was examined and given a strong sedative with a recommendation to see a psychiatrist soon. The police allowed Fisher to give his statement at home.

The cop who took his statement had been one of the first ones at the scene.

"We'll try to keep certain details quiet from the media," the cop assured him, labouring to keep a straight face. For as long as he lived, he would never forget that scene, seeing the prominent business-man bent over his bed, his pants at his ankles, with a gay gunman behind him, ready to do the deed, whilst the man's tied up wife watched in terror.

Fisher nodded gratefully, his traumatized, partially bandaged face looking every bit of its forty-nine years. They were finished but the cop hesitated, waiting to see if Fisher would offer him some money. No such offer was forthcoming.

"So..." the cop began, "seeing as we arrived in such a timely manner and saved you from an experience that would have probably driven you insane...don't you think a little reward would be appropriate?"

Fisher glared at the cop for a long moment before abruptly going into his bedroom. That fucking piece of shit. Wanting to get paid for doing his job. Beulah, his helper, was the real hero. She was still in the house when he had entered with the intruder. She was about to take his ironed shirts to his room when she had seen the man behind him, holding a gun to his head, as they walked down the hallway. After being frozen in shock for a few seconds, she had sprung into action and called the police. To their credit they had responded quickly. Perfect timing in fact. He didn't know what he would have done had they arrived later and that man had...he couldn't bear to think about it.

He returned with a brown envelope and handed it brusquely to the cop.

The cop thanked him, a tiny smirk playing at the corner of his lips, and left the house. He didn't look inside the envelope until he was in the car, where his partner was waiting. Twenty thousand dollars. He frowned. He saved this man from getting fucked up the ass and he only gave him twenty thousand dollars. The cop sucked his teeth. He wished they had gotten there five minutes later. He chuckled at the thought and gave his partner eight thousand out of the money. They then headed out to the station.

The businessman's near rape was the joke of the night.

CR...SOCR...SO

The incident was big news the following morning. It made the front pages of two of the nation's top newspapers and it was mentioned on every radio talk show. Yanique couldn't believe it. Her grandmother had called her early in the morning, waking her up, to tell her what had happened. Despite knowing about the situation, the surprise she had expressed was genuine as she hadn't expected any bloodshed much less somebody dying. She had thought that he would have pulled off the robbery, gotten a good amount of money and other valuables, and that would have been that.

The fact that he was gay was also a big shocker. Now she understood why he had been so upset at her when she told him about her intimate relationship with Marilyn Dell-Fisher. His conscience had gotten the better of him. She was sorry that he had died, but perhaps it was all for the best. If he had been captured alive he would have probably fingered her as an accomplice and brought her down with him. Her heartbeat became irregular at the thought. Her whole life would have been turned upside down because of her gay cousin. It had been a close call. She had told Justine and Shari that Double Ugly was going to come and see her, and deal with Fisher for her. She would have to tell them, especially Justine, who was a bit on the garrulous side, not to breathe a word of that to anyone.

CR...SOCR...SO

Karim went to pick up Olivia when he left the office at 6:30 p.m. that evening. It took him over an hour to get to Armour Heights from Oxford Road. The evening traffic with people heading uptown after work was atrocious. When he finally got there, he chatted with Taj and Alondra for a few minutes then left with Olivia. She carried all her luggage as she would not be coming back to the house before heading to the airport tomorrow.

She slipped off her Gucci sandals, reclined her seat a bit and placed her small, pretty feet on the dashboard. Karim didn't mind, though the view of her legs and her provocative pose was distracting. She was wearing tiny white shorts and a black Diesel tank top with a black and white Chanel scarf tied around her lengthy mane. She looked hot even when she wasn't trying. She just couldn't help it.

"How was your day *papacito*?" she asked, her brown-green eyes peering at him from underneath her long lashes. They were the longest, real set of lashes he had ever seen. God was really paying attention when he made her.

Karim cursed as a taxi-man, anxious to dump his passengers and pick up another load, overtook a line of traffic and zipped in front of him without warning, causing him to brake suddenly. He was grateful that he managed to avoid a collision. It would have been a rotten stroke of luck for him to hit the car at this juncture, seeing as it was practically sold. It was just a matter for the guy to put the money in his account and that would be done on Friday morning. He had already given his friend a fifty percent deposit on the Dodge Ram and it would be licensed and insured tomorrow. He was depending on the money from the sale of the car to complete the payment for the Ram.

"*Pelotudo!*" Olivia exclaimed in annoyance, her luminous eyes flashing, as she was unceremoniously flung forward. "Dumbass!"

"You ok?" Karim asked, looking over at her concerned.

She winced but smiled. "Yeah *papacito*...there's a slight pain in my right side...guess I twisted it a bit but I'm ok."

Karim slightly raised her top and lightly caressed her side as they waited for the light to turn green.

"Mmmm...don't get me started papi...you know I'll take your dick out and suck it right now so be careful how you're touching me," she warned, a devilish look on her beautiful face.

Karim laughed heartily.

Olivia was something else.

He was going to miss her.

Chapter 15

Shari sucked her teeth in annoyance as the disheveled young man, disregarding her instructions that he should not touch her vehicle, started to wipe her windshield with a filthy sponge. She sprayed her wiper fluid and turned on the wipers. He stopped and glared at her angrily.

"Yuh can't just gimme a fifty dolla nice girl? Eh?" he asked, his putrid body odour causing her to quickly close the window.

That made him angry. He threw his bucket of dirty water on her vehicle, telling her some choice words as he stood on the divider in the middle of the road.

Shari was incensed. Her sparklingly clean vehicle was now a mess because of this disgusting asshole who was acting like she owed him something. She wished she had a licensed firearm. She would wipe that smirk right off his ugly, dirty face.

She was on Trafalgar Road in the slow-moving Friday evening traffic. She was heading up to Shades Café to meet the girls for karaoke and drinks.

Shari watched in shock as a man grabbed the youth and slapped him twice before hauling him unceremoniously over to her vehicle. It was Karim.

Shari, her mouth a wide O, lowered her window.

"Apologize to the lady," Karim told the embarrassed youth. People in the traffic honked their horns in approval; several of them most likely having suffered abuse from the ill-mannered brutes that plagued motorists at most stoplights in the corporate area.

"Sorry, Miss," the lad, who didn't look a day over seventeen said reluctantly, his surly face stinging mightily from the hearty slaps that Karim had given him.

Karim then shoved him away after warning him to mark her face and look the other way whenever he saw her in the future.

"My knight in shining armour," Shari teased, thoroughly impressed by what she just saw. "Thanks but you didn't have to do that."

"I was over there in the adjacent lane when I realized it was you that punk was messing with." Karim's eyes skimmed over her fitted grey trousers and black sleeveless top. A black blazer was on the passenger seat along with a black Prada tote bag.

The traffic was beginning to crawl a few more inches.

"Well that was really nice of you...now you need to get back to your vehicle," she told him with a smile.

He whipped out his phone as he climbed back inside his truck. He drove up and was now right beside her. He watched as she retrieved her phone and answered it. He could see her looking into her side mirror for his car.

"You still have my number," she stated, inexplicably pleased that he had kept it.

"You still have my attention," he replied. "So it's only fair."

"I wasn't aware that I had your attention Mr. Dawkins," she said.

"Wipe that smirk off your face," Karim told her.

"What smirk?" Shari asked laughing, looking around for him.

"I'm right beside you," Karim told her, winding down his tinted window.

Shari had to look up to see him. Her eyes conveyed her surprise.

"You have changed your vehicle," she said, "very nice. Suits you."

"Thanks, yeah I just picked it up today."

The traffic moved again and Shari ended up two vehicles ahead.

"Look, Shari, I'd really like to spend some time with you...get to know you better," he said.

Shari didn't respond immediately. *Here it comes.* It was tempting but no. She couldn't go there. If she entertained his advances and acted upon her own interest, they would definitely get involved and then what? He would die, just like the rest of them and leave her heartbroken and feeling like the grim reaper.

"I'm sorry but I'm not interested," she told him bluntly.

Karim recoiled in his seat like she had physically slapped him.

He was temporarily at a loss for words.

"Thanks but no thanks," she went on mercilessly. "Enjoy the weekend and take care."

It took a few moments before Karim realized that she had ended the call.

He lit a cigarette and drove up as the traffic inched forward a few meters. *Damn she was a cold fish.* But that was what he deserved. He had already told himself that he would not pursue her yet here he was playing himself. He felt stupid. He grabbed the remote control for the CD player and selected disc 3. The sounds of Young Jeezy's album *The Recession* filtered through the Bose speakers.

She had confirmed what he had already suspected. She didn't want him. He took a deep drag and sighed out a cloud of smoke. *Well fuck it. It was her loss.* He would be going to Miami in two weeks to attend

Taj's birthday party. He was looking forward to seeing Olivia and she was even more excited that he was coming.

Fuck Shari.

Olivia was hotter anyway.

If that was true why did it sound hollow to his ears?

CR...ROCR...RO

Shari felt bad about what she had just done. Angry even. She wanted him too. Life was so unfair. But it was for the best. She didn't think that she could live with herself if she ever gave in and something happened to him. She sighed in frustration. It had been almost a week since her experience with the lawyer who suffered from premature ejaculation. That prick. She had someone in mind to give a chance but this time she wouldn't just jump into bed with him. She would hang out with him from time to time and have some casual fun before giving him a piece of the pie.

Maybe a fuck buddy would work out better than a one night stand. The guy she had in mind was a creative consultant with the Ministry of Culture. She had met him sometime ago and though she had taken his number, had never given him a call. She called him earlier today and he had remembered her right off the bat. She accepted his invitation to attend a jazz show on Saturday night. Her mind drifted back to Karim. It was so sexy the way he had disciplined that street guy. Nothing dramatic or pretentious, he just handled it like a man. Turned her on like crazy. She sighed and tried to brush aside the unwelcome thoughts.

Pining over what might have been was useless.

She was saving his life, though he didn't know it.

And besides, after the way she just rejected him, she was sure he would never speak to her again.

Chapter 16

"Papacito!" Olivia gushed as she hugged Karim tightly, oblivious of the stares that she was attracting. "I'm so happy to see you."

Karim grinned as she kissed him. He had arrived in Miami an hour ago and just cleared customs. Taj, Alondra and Olivia had come to pick him up.

He greeted Taj and Alondra while Olivia, draped all over him like a second skin, stuck her tongue out at Taj when he wondered out loud if she wasn't going to give the man space to breathe. They loaded his lone piece of luggage into Taj's white Cadillac Escalade and headed out.

Taj and Karim have been best friends since they met at preparatory school at age six. Taj was an American by birth; his mother had lived in Maryland at the time when she was pregnant with him. Taj's mom had met his dad in Las Vegas while they were both there on vacation. His dad had been there with his family – his wife and two kids, and his mother had been there with three of her friends, enjoying two weeks of fun after they had all graduated from the same University.

Their well to do parents had sent the three close friends on the trip as a graduation present. Taj's mom, a young attractive twenty year old at the time, had met the charming, white forty year old diplomat at the roulette table in one of the casinos on the strip. The attraction had been immediate, and the diplomat had sent home his family early so that he could spend as much time as possible with the sexy Jamaican woman that he just couldn't get enough of.

Taj had been the result of the torrid affair which didn't end until his father's death from acute lymphoblastic leukemia when Taj was nineteen. Even when his mother had gotten involved in a serious relationship because she was tired of waiting for him to divorce his wife, they still had an intimate relationship. Taj's twelve year old half sister, Laci, was the product of that union. Taj's father had provided well for them, and the house that Taj owned in Miami had been willed to him by his dad.

Taj's birthday party was tonight. He was having it at a popular bar and lounge on Purdy Avenue in Miami Beach. Taj, who was also a popular DJ in the

Miami party scene, was well-known and the party would be well attended. A few local celebrities, including a Miami Heat forward, models and several rappers were expected to be there.

Karim had come on the earliest possible flight so that he would have time to do some shopping. They were heading to the Bal Harbour Shops, considered to be the most exclusive shopping destination in the southern United States. They parked and joined the throng of well-dressed shoppers strolling through the pleasant open-air emporium. The theme for the party was *Gents in Gucci, Dames in Dior.* They glanced at the store directory and headed over to the Gucci store. Karim had told Taj a few days ago not to buy his outfit yet as he would get him one as a birthday gift.

They entered the swanky Gucci store and a young lady dressed in a black pleated knee-length skirt with thin black stockings and a white ruffle blouse, came to their assistance. Karim purchased a pair of black hi-top sneakers, the matching belt, grey jeans and a red and black cardigan. Taj, in choosing his gift, selected blue jeans, black loafers and a fitted black army style shirt.

Next was the Dior store to get something for the girls. It was a couple doors down between the Salvatore Ferragamo and Max Mara stores. Karim bought silver leggings, a white baby doll top with an empire waist and black stilettos for a beaming Olivia, while Taj, not to be outdone, purchased a black belted twill sheath dress and metallic purple leather detail pumps for Alondra.

Lunch at the Zodiac Café on the third floor of Neiman Marcus was next. They lunched on crab cakes; oven broiled rainbow trout with roasted almonds and lemon juice; and jumbo grilled shrimp with eggplant caviar.

An hour and a half later, Taj dropped off Karim and Olivia at Olivia's loft in Coral Gables that she shared with Alondra, but with Alondra staying with Taj, they would have the place to themselves. After promising to pick them up at 10, Taj and Alondra headed to his home in Aventura. He had hired someone to deal with the preparations for the party as the last thing he needed was to be stressed out dealing with all the planning and details. He had conceptualized everything and given his instructions weeks ago and everything was going according to plan. All he had to do was show up and enjoy his twenty-sixth birthday.

CR...❦CR...❦

"*Muchas gracias* for a wonderful day *papacito*," Olivia told him as she slowly undressed him. "I feel like it's *my* birthday."

Karim laughed. He had spent close to seven thousand dollars today. That was a lot of money to blow in these tight times but with his mobile car wash doing well and his fifty percent stake in the car dealership and T-shirt business, he could afford to splurge every now and then.

"You're welcome baby," he replied, losing himself inside her sparkling brown-green eyes. She was very happy to see him. He could see the joy in her eyes. It felt good. Shari's blunt rejection over two weeks ago had hurt him more than he would like to admit. Having the beautiful and utterly delectable Latina so into him was helping a great deal to soothe his bruised ego.

"*Te extrano mucho*," she murmured as she nibbled on his bottom lip, making him moan softly. "Very, very much."

Karim was guessing that she was telling him how much she missed him.

"Show me," he breathed, his eyes glazed like donuts.

She pulled him down to the carpeted floor and did just that in several ways for the next hour.

Chapter 17

Shari yawned and closed the book she was reading. It was the autobiography of one of her idols, Michelle Obama. She was halfway through it but it was getting late and her eyes were tired. She placed the book on the bedside table and switched off the lamp. A wee bit of moonlight filtered in from the slightly open window. She curled up with one of the pillows between her legs and closed her eyes.

She had gotten a call over the weekend from the director of a rival advertising agency. Apparently he had heard great things about her and wanted her to come and work for him. He told her that whatever she was currently getting he would add 50% to that along with incentives and perks. Shari was flattered and though she had no intentions of leaving her current job, she told him to give her some time to think about it. Sometimes one should keep their options open.

Karim crossed her mind, as he tended to do from to time, before she fell asleep. She was still feeling him though she had shut him down without ever giving him a chance. She constantly had to reassure herself that she had done the right thing.

But how could something that was right feel so wrong?

CR…ဢOCR…ဢO

Karim placed his luggage in the closet and quickly undressed. He was dead tired. He had just gotten back to Jamaica on the last flight out of Miami. He had called two of his friends to see if they could come and pick him up but their phones had gone straight to voicemail so he had taken a cab home. He'd had a blast this weekend.

Taj's party had been off the chain and spending time with Olivia had been great. If she had only liked him a great deal before this weekend, she was now absolutely in love with him. He liked her, liked her a lot, but surprisingly, he wasn't in love with her. Something, or rather someone, was preventing his heart from fully opening up to Olivia.

Shari.

It angered and frustrated him but it was true.

Olivia was as close to perfection as a woman could get yet he still wanted someone who didn't want him.

Life could really be a menstruating bitch sometimes.

Chapter 18

Where do I know this guy from? Justine mused, as she pushed the trolley down the canned goods aisle. She looked at him as she picked up a can of green peas and a can of sweet corn. She was at Shop Smart, a supermarket in Liguanea, picking up a few items before heading home. Then she remembered. Super bowl Sunday. At the sports bar in Kingston. He had been there with a group of people. She watched as he picked up a couple cans of salmon. She continued down the aisle towards him.

"Hi," she said, a coy smile lurking at the corners of her thin lips.

Karim turned to look at her.

"Hey," he replied, with a questioning look.

"I saw you at the sports bar in New Kingston in late January and I remembered you immediately...

guess you made quite an impression..." she purred, playing with her hair.

"I see," Karim replied nonchalantly.

"So...I think you're really hot and I would love to hang out with you some time," she stated boldly, looking directly into his eyes.

Karim looked her over critically before responding. She was attractive enough, interesting if not pretty face, long legs and a pert pair of breasts.

"Is that right," he drawled, in the same non-committal tone.

"Yes it is," Justine pressed. "Are you interested?"

"Give me your number," Karim told her, checking his watch. It was Thursday night and that meant a NBA doubleheader on TNT. The first game started in forty-five minutes. He needed to go. "I'll call you."

Justine was a bit peeved at his lack of enthusiasm but she gave him the number.

"Ok, guess I'll hear from you soon," she said, giving him a seductive look before heading back down the aisle. She adopted her best runway walk and when she reached the end of the aisle, she looked back to see if he had enjoyed the show.

He wasn't there.

Only an obese Indian man with his trolley, ironically filled with fresh fruits and vegetables, was in the aisle.

He smiled at her and winked.

Justine cut her eyes at him and haughtily made her way to the cashier.

As if.

CR...℘℘CR...℘℘

"What a bum...can't believe he gets paid millions to do that shit every night," Shari commented disgustedly, as she watched an overpaid – at least in her and a lot of sports writers estimation – Dallas Mavericks player miss a point blank lay up. She was at home watching the first of a NBA double-header on TNT.

Yanique was there with her, half-watching as she browsed the internet on Shari's cute red Dell laptop. She was on You Tube checking out the latest video clips. She had been back to work for three weeks now and had yet to see or speak to her boss, who she was told was on extended leave. Even now the robbery, shooting and near rape that had happened at her home was still the biggest gossip at the large bank. Everyone speculated that she wouldn't come back to work. Yanique was told by Jean, a garrulous thirty year old that had a flatulence problem, who also worked in the personal banking department, that Mrs. Dell-Fisher and her husband were vacationing in Europe after their traumatic experience. Thankfully, no one had gotten wind of the fact that Yanique had been having an affair with Mrs. Dell-Fisher and that the husband had caught them in bed together.

127

Yanique chuckled as she looked at a video that a teenage girl from Sweden had posted of her attempting to do the latest Jamaican dance moves. Her cousin, Double Ugly, had been buried a couple days ago – she didn't attend the funeral and her face was now pretty much back to normal. As was her life. She had put the whole sordid mess behind her.

"So what's up with that guy you met the other day?" Shari asked, looking over at Yanique.

"Who...the one at work?" Yanique queried, looking up.

Shari nodded. During a telephone conversation a few nights ago Yanique had told her that she liked the new teller.

"Oh," Yanique said, scrunching up her face and waving her hand dismissively. "I'm no longer interested ...his dick is physically challenged."

Shari chuckled. "What do you mean?"

"Shari that shit is so tiny...you'd have to see it to believe it."

"Damn!" Shari exclaimed. "You gave him some?"

"Nope...I was planning to but we were in the parking lot yesterday talking by his car and I felt him up...and girl, I almost fainted in disbelief. Such a shame. Very nice looking guy."

Shari laughed. Yanique was something else. She was so aggressive. She could only imagine the shock on the poor guy's face when Yanique grabbed his dick in the middle of their conversation.

"You never know though Yanique...some of those tiny ones grow really large once it gets hard..."

Yanique looked at her with a serious expression. "It was hard. I had been telling him how good I was going to suck his dick."

Shari laughed heartily. She hoped she didn't have any such problem this weekend. She had been seeing a lot of the creative consultant over the past few weeks and she enjoyed his company. Though there wasn't any great physical attraction on her part – she had yet to even kiss him on the lips – she planned to give him some this weekend. She was unbelievably horny. It was time to give him the fuck buddy test. She hoped that he would give a good account of himself. Lord knows she needed some good dick.

She turned her attention back to the game.

ᘓ...ᘓᘓ...ᘓ

"Hello," Karim said, as he answered the phone while keeping his eyes glued to the game. The second game of the double-header had started and the Lakers had started the game on a 10-0 run, capped by a Kobe Bryant tomahawk dunk.

"Hi Karim, it's me," Kimberly said timidly. It was her first time speaking to him since that night when she slammed his car door and stormed inside her house. She had held out for as long as she could but she missed him terribly. Whatever terms she had to accept in order to be in his life, she would. There was just this terrible ache inside her that wouldn't go away until he became a part of her life again.

Karim sighed. She had called from a private number so he hadn't known who was calling. If he had had any idea that it was her, he wouldn't have answered the phone. Kimberly was drama that he didn't need. He liked her well enough, to have fun with, but not to play the girlfriend role that she so badly wanted to play. And he had made that perfectly clear.

"What do you want Kimberly?" he asked coldly.

"I miss you Karim," she said, ignoring his freezing tone.

Karim remained silent as he watched Lamar Odom get into an argument with an opposing player that had committed a hard foul on him underneath the basket. Players from both teams along with the referees tried to separate the players before things escalated into a fight.

Kimberly pressed on. "I know you don't want anything more than a casual relationship and I've accepted that. I can't force you to make me your girl-friend but I do miss and want you...so I'll accept just being your friend with benefits."

Karim mulled that over silently.

"Are you sure? I don't want to hear that now and then a couple weeks down the line you start whining that you want more," he responded tersely.

"I'm sure Karim," she said softly, thankful that he couldn't see her tears. Why didn't he want her? She was hot. She could dress her ass off. She was freaky in bed. Her family had a prominent name. "Seriously... we won't have that problem again. I mean I still want you for myself but I won't make an issue out of it. I swear."

After a pregnant pause, Karim agreed to see her again.

They made plans to see each other over the weekend and Karim hung up and went back to watching the game.

Kimberly went to bed.

She touched herself.

She was wet.

Just knowing that she was going to see Karim soon was enough to make her drench her panties.

She hated him.

She wanted him.

She hated that she wanted him.

Chapter 19

On Saturday night, after knocking back a few martinis with Leon, the creative consultant, at a trendy new night spot on Trinidad Terrace, Shari accepted his invitation to go back to his place. The moon was full, the night cool and starry, and she was slightly tipsy and horny. There was no way in hell that she was going home to hug up her pillow tonight. She needed to get laid.

They arrived at Leon's townhouse on Swansea Avenue twenty minutes after leaving the club. Shari looked around his home as she sat on the couch and removed her red Miu Miu pumps. His place was nice enough, very masculine in dark contrasting hues which showed that his creativity wasn't left at the office. Smiling broadly, he led her by hand to the bedroom. Shari noticed his use of contrasting floor textures to act as an invisible divider between living spaces. The living room had ceramic tiling while the bedroom had a wooden floor.

Leon didn't waste any time once they got to the bedroom. He switched on the bedside lamp and undressed quickly. Shari hoped fervently that wasn't a sign of things to come. She watched keenly as he removed his grey boxer-briefs. He passed the first test. His semi-erect dick was thick but it was the oddest looking dick she had ever seen. It had a weird shape. It was almost triangular: narrow at the head and progressively wider all the way down to the base.

What the fuck? This should be interesting, Shari mused, as she followed suit and slipped out of her little black Max Mara dress. Her thong followed quickly. She hadn't worn a bra.

Leon said something she couldn't quite make out as he advanced towards her with lust-filled eyes. His triangular-looking dick was now fully erect. Shari couldn't wait to see how it would feel inside her. He pulled her to him and they kissed for the first time. He was a good kisser. Shari moaned. He explored her mouth passionately as he caressed and groped her pert ass. She spread her legs and placed his right hand at the center of her heat. He used his palm to caress her plump mound before slipping one finger inside her wetness.

"Ohhh...yeah..." Shari moaned as he fingered her and sucked on her nipples.

She was ready.

Fuck the foreplay.

She pushed him away.

"Get a condom on and come over here and fuck me like you'll never have the chance to do it again," Shari told him wantonly as she climbed onto his bed and spread her legs, her plump pussy crying erotic tears. She was soaking wet. "Hurry up!"

Leon couldn't believe Shari's transformation. The sexy but always ladylike beauty had no qualms about telling a man what she wanted once they were inside the bedroom. He ripped away the gold wrapping of a Trojan Magnum and sheathed his sword. He got on top of her and placed it at the entrance of her pulsating orifice.

"Give it to me," Shari urged as he entered her slowly.

It was the weirdest sensation ever.

At first she didn't feel anything, and then, as he slowly went deeper, it felt like her pussy walls were being forced apart.

"Fucking hell...oh God...it feels so thick...fuck!" Shari grunted through clenched teeth, as he pulled all the way out before pushing it back in all the way to the hilt, wracking Shari's body with that weird sensation over and over again.

The feeling was unlike anything she'd ever experienced.

Leon increased his tempo, drilling Shari until her moans became screams.

"You think I can't take it huh?" Shari challenged between her screams. "You think I can't handle your thick retarded dick? Fuck me! Break it off inside me!"

Leon attempted to do just that.

CR...ᏕᎧCR...ᏕᎧ

"Damn I missed you..." Kimberly breathed.

Karim wasn't sure who she was talking about, him or his dick.

She had it cradled in her soft, manicured hands, massaging it with her lips and tongue languidly, savouring its lengthy thickness, running her tongue along the bulging veins. It was so hard. She took it deep in her mouth, her head bobbing fiercely as she sucked him hard, making him groan in ecstasy.

Karim had made her drive to his apartment – a first as he used to always pick her up – and they had devoured half a bottle of Hennessy while listening to Kanye West's latest album, before she had pulled his dick out and started showing him just how much she had missed it.

"I missed this sweet juicy dick...mmmm...mmmm ...so perfect..." she breathed as she sucked him noisily; her slurps louder than Kanye West's auto tune wailings that he had employed for most of the album.

Kimberly then retrieved a condom and used her knowledgeable mouth to roll it onto his dick. Karim got behind her and entered her with a hard thrust. Kimberly grabbed a cushion and bit into it savagely, as a pleasurable jolt of pain travelled from her pussy to her brain and back again. His strokes were hard and relentless, pounding her into orgasmic submission as she climaxed over and over again. When he was finally through forty-five minutes later, she was sore and unable to move.

Karim had enjoyed it, but the pleasure was fleeting. Now as he lay on his back and lit a cigarette, he felt dissatisfied. Unfulfilled. Wanting. Something was missing. Apparently emotionless sex wasn't as enjoyable for him like it used to be.

And he knew why.

Shari.

Goddamn that girl.

First she was preventing him from fully committing to a beautiful woman who worshipped the ground he walked on and now she was messing with his sex life.

The fact that she was blissfully unaware of what she was doing to him did nothing to lessen the frustration.

He was going to have to do something about this. And soon.

CR...SOCR...SO

Shari locked the door and leaned against it in frustration. Leon had just dropped her home. After nearly an hour of sex, she had been unable to have an orgasm. Leon had tremendous stamina but he just could not make her climax from penetration. Maybe his weird shaped dick was the problem, she wasn't sure, but the bottom line was, she didn't come. He had offered to eat her until she did but she had declined and asked him to drop her home instead.

She trudged to the bathroom, stripped off her clothes and took a warm shower.

Another meaningless sexual encounter gone awry.

Another man had gotten her body and left her feeling empty and frustrated afterwards.

No more. She couldn't do this anymore. It wasn't working out for her and besides, fucking someone who didn't mean anything to her was simply not her cup of tea. She wasn't a promiscuous girl by nature. Up until Nicholas' death, she had only been intimate with four men and they had all been serious relationships. Now she had quickly added two more to the list and it hadn't been worth it. What was she supposed to do? Continue to fuck strange men and feel cheap and unfulfilled afterwards? Or be in a nice, stable monogamous relationship and watch the man she cared for die a tragic death? It had happened four times straight. Who's to say it wouldn't happen again?

She was damned if she did and damned if she didn't.

She turned the shower off and got out. She dried herself and padded to the bedroom where she moisturized her body with her favourite lotion. She then slipped on a T-shirt and climbed into bed. She turned the radio on and pulled the covers over her head.

She was confused and frustrated.

She couldn't continue like this.

But she didn't know what to do.

Her heart was telling her to give Karim a chance and let the chips fall where they may. Her heart was a hypocrite. It had been put through the wringer on four consecutive occasions and now it was telling her to put it on the line again. Yeah right. And besides, even if she decided to give Karim a chance he might no longer be available or he might be, but wasn't interested in her anymore. After how she had dealt with him the last time they had spoken, she wouldn't be surprised if that was the case. She could feel a tension headache coming on.

She tried to stop thinking so much and willed herself to sleep.

Chapter 20

Aiesha finished up with the customer and put the phone down. Her mind was on her boss. He hadn't been the same lately. Seemed a bit sad. He hadn't even fucked her in awhile. She wondered what was wrong with him. She glanced up at the clock on the wall to her right. It was almost closing time. She wondered if he wanted her to do anything to make him feel better. Five minutes later, she locked the front door and walked down to his office. She knocked on the door lightly.

"Come," she heard gruffly from inside.

She opened the door and went in, closing it behind her.

She looked at him, feeling a bit nervous. Karim could be very cold when he was ready and she didn't want him to embarrass her.

"Everything ok boss?" she asked, sitting on one of the two chairs in front of his desk.

Karim closed the file on his desk and leaned back in his chair.

"Yeah," he finally responded after a few seconds. "Just have some things on my mind."

"Anything I can do to help?" she asked softly, her pussy already wet, hoping he'd say yes.

Karim looked at his computer screen. The screen saver was the company logo that Taj had designed. He sighed. Business was going well, especially in light of the economic crunch going on worldwide. Even the car dealership was still doing well. In hindsight, his decision to overrule his partner and focus on specializing in only cheap, affordable cars had paid off. They were thriving while other car dealerships were wondering how much longer they'd be able to stay in business.

The T-shirt line was doing well, more and more celebrities in Miami were endorsing the line. Taj would be coming down in three weeks. They were going to launch their new designs in Kingston. The summer was only three months away and they wanted their T-shirts to be the must have gear for the summer. Based on the hot new designs that Taj had come up with, Karim was certain that they would be a hit.

Only one thing wasn't going well.

His personal life.

He had been agonizing for the past two weeks about the best way to approach Shari. He had her contact information on the business card that she had given to him at the time of the accident but he didn't want to call, text or email her, and though he knew where her office was located, he didn't want to just pop up at her workplace like that. He was also afraid of another rejection. He already felt stupid for still feeling so strongly about someone that he didn't really know and who had made it emphatically clear that she wasn't interested.

It was affecting him so badly that he hadn't even had sex all week.

Maybe a good fuck from Aiesha would help to take the edge off.

"Come here," he said.

She smiled broadly and quickly made her way around his desk.

CR...SOCR...SO

"Working late tonight?" Mr. Carter asked Shari as he walked by her spacious cubicle, which was the closest one to his office. She was sitting around her computer, typing.

Shari looked up, a tired half-smile on her cute face.

"Not very late...just finishing up the proposal for the meeting with Khan and Associates."

Mr. Carter nodded approvingly. They didn't make employees like Shari any more. For someone so young, she was one of the hardest working and most mature persons he knew. She had recently told him about the offer from their competitor but had told him not to worry, as she wasn't going anywhere. He was very touched by her loyalty. He couldn't match the 50% pay hike that they had offered but he had given her a 25% increase with a promise of more when the economy turned around.

Loyalty.

Who knew people still had that trait?

"Ok Shari, see you tomorrow."

Shari waved bye and resumed her typing.

He looked at her for a moment longer as a paternal feeling came over him. He could only hope that his daughter would turn out to be such a nice, well-rounded young woman. He then made his way out to the parking lot.

Shari's stomach uttered a very unladylike growl; startling her. She chuckled, embarrassed though she was by herself. She glanced at the time. It was 7 p.m. She was hungry and there wasn't anything at the house to eat that she wouldn't have to cook. She wasn't in the mood for that. As soon as she finished working she would head over to Ribs Delight and get some dinner.

CR...SOCR...SO

Ribs Delight was a trendy eatery on Knutsford Boulevard. The owner, a Texan who had fallen in love with Jamaica, imported only the best steak and tie that in with an excellent chef, a delicious secret sauce, and the best customer service in town, Ribs Delight was a hit. Eating there was an expensive venture, but it was worth every penny.

Shari got there at 8:15 and made her way over to one of the vacant booths. She was famished. A waitress quickly came over, and with a smile that gave no indication that she had been on her feet since midday, took Shari's order.

Shari ordered the Dallas Cowboys – the owner, a huge sports fan, had various meals named after his favourite sports teams – which consisted of an extra thick cut 30 oz. prime rib served with bacon wrapped scallops and huge French fries.

She looked around as she waited for her meal. The place had a nice sized crowd for a Wednesday night. She could see the door from where she was sitting and watched as the door man politely dealt with a belligerent man who wanted to dine there wearing an Ed Hardy tank top. Tank tops were not allowed. The man, who sounded American, cursed the door man out whilst the door man, who had biceps the size of truck tires, politely but firmly kept him outside.

Shari fiddled with her Blackberry, checking her email and looking at her notes for the next few minutes until the waitress thankfully returned with her food.

Shari dug into her food with restrained gusto. It was so good that she smiled as she ate. The smile froze on her face when she saw Karim enter the restaurant. He was about to go over to the take-out section when he felt her eyes and looked over where she was sitting.

Oh God! Please don't let him come over here! Shari prayed silently, her face flushed with embarrassment at the way she had behaved the last time they had spoken and the fluttering in her stomach at the sight of him. Apparently God was taking a nap. After a moment's hesitation, Karim made his way towards her.

Shari's heart raced.

She willed herself to calm down.

"Mind if I sit?" he asked, as he stood by the table looking down at her.

She didn't look up at him. Her food was suddenly the most interesting thing she had ever seen. Her eyes were glued to her plate even as she shook her head.

Karim sat.

She could smell his cologne.

Amen by Thierry Mugler.

Her favourite scent to smell on a man.

"I'd love to know where all your food goes..." he teased.

She finally raised her eyes and looked at him.

He looked so fucking hot sitting there in his designer Obama T-shirt covered with a black army style jacket she just wanted to swap him for the steak and eat him up.

She gave him a mock glower.

"Wouldn't you like to know..." she said coyly.

"That I would," he countered, giving her a look that turned her body into an inferno.

Shari quickly placed some food in her mouth to distract her. Why did he have to come to the restaurant and see her? She wasn't prepared for this. She wasn't prepared for his intoxicating nearness, his sexy voice, the way he licked his lips unconsciously. Her body was going through more reactions than a chemistry experiment.

"I've been thinking about you a lot," he told her, looking straight in her eyes. She tried to look away but couldn't. She felt hypnotized. "I know that you said that you're not interested but I don't believe you. And I'm not taking no for an answer. My happiness is too important to me."

Shari was stunned.

"I meant it," she said, after a prolonged silence, sounding unconvincing to her own ears. "And besides...what do I have to with your happiness?"

He suddenly leaned forward and holding on to her jacket by the lapels, pulled her to him and kissed her on the lips forcefully.

"Everything," he said, breaking the kiss and getting up leaving a stunned Shari wondering why she felt like she was levitating above the table instead of sitting down. Her face crimson, she suddenly remembered to breathe. Letting out a deep breath, she resumed eating like nothing had happened. She didn't dare look around. She just *knew* that people were watching her.

Goddamn Karim.

Who the hell did he think he was?

The man who can turn me into a river by just his mere presence.

Shari wondered since when her pussy could talk.

Chapter 21

Thursday was a weird day for Shari. She was unable to fully concentrate on work and she was filled with conflicting emotions. Seeing Karim last night had thrown her into an emotional tailspin. And that kiss. That hot, demanding, forceful unexpected kiss that had made her forget to breathe. The brief but memorable kiss was packed with more ingredients than a full house pizza.

Passion. Lust. Want. Need. Frustration. Longing.

She had felt it all. And it both scared and excited her to no end. Why couldn't he leave her alone? Why didn't she want him to leave her alone?

She felt like a confused teenager.

I want him, I want him not.

She sighed and looked at the time. It was 11:45. She was supposed to be meeting with Yanique for lunch at 12. She badly needed someone to talk to and she preferred to confide in Yanique about matters of the heart more than Justine. Justine had a way of turning everything into a joke and this was no laughing matter. Yanique was a free spirit when it came to relationships but she was a good listener, and that was what Shari needed.

Though she had been telling herself all morning that Karim had better not call her and if he did, she wouldn't answer, she was disappointed that he hadn't.

She picked up her Louis Vuitton pocketbook and was about to head out when the receptionist called out to her. Shari went over to the desk.

"A bearer just delivered this for you," she said, smiling questioningly as though she expected Shari to divulge her personal business.

Though her heart had done two back flips when she took the long slender white box with the pink ribbon from the receptionist's outstretched hand, her face remained stoic.

"Thank you," she said and quickly made her way out to the parking lot.

She went inside her vehicle and switched on the engine, turning the AC on full blast in an attempt to cool herself down. It had to be from Karim. She was mildly annoyed at how excited she had become. What the hell was this guy doing to her?

She opened the box.

It contained a single pink orchid. It was beautiful. There was a note attached.

Orchids represent love, luxury, strength and beauty. The pink orchid, in particular, conveys pure affection. Have a great day my future.

Karim

Shari leaned back in her seat. This was so sweet. She really should call him and tell him thanks. No, she shouldn't call. A thank you note would be more appropriate. Or maybe she shouldn't say anything at all. Christ. If she didn't get herself together soon this situation was going to drive her crazy. She sighed and placed the flower on the passenger seat.

She then headed out for her lunch date with Yanique.

CR...SOCR...SO

"*Papacito*...I have something to tell you," Olivia said.

Karim was at his office, just about to dive into his Chinese take-out, when Olivia rang him on his mobile. She sounded distraught. Karim put his fork down and leaned back in his comfortable leather swivel chair. His extension was beeping but he ignored it. Whatever Aiesha wanted could wait.

"What is it babes?" Karim asked earnestly.

"I-I-I'm pregnant," she whispered hoarsely.

Karim was stunned. But they had always used condoms!

"It's not for you...the guy that I was seeing...it's his..." she continued.

Karim's breathing returned to normal. When she told him the first thing that crossed his mind was that it would complicate things with Shari. Make it even harder for him to get her to come around.

"I had stopped sleeping with him after I met you but one evening he came over to see me and forced me to have sex with him," she went on. "I struggled with him Papacito...I really did but gave up when he started to get really violent. I took a morning after pill but apparently it didn't work. I'm three weeks pregnant. *Lo siento.*"

"Damn boo...I'm so sorry to hear that," Karim responded. "That's really fucked up."

"Yeah...he did it on purpose...to tie me to him forever," Olivia cried. She blew her nose, composed herself and continued. "*Papacito...*I'm Catholic and I don't believe in abortion...but I'll get rid of it if that's what you want...I'll do it for you."

Karim's heart sank. This girl loved him so much. But his heart was somewhere else. It was unclaimed, but it was somewhere else, waiting impatiently for the owner to realize that it was hers. Maybe this was a blessing in disguise. He had been wondering how he was going to cut ties with Olivia without hurting her when Shari finally decided to give things a chance.

"No baby...I would never ask you to do that," Karim responded softly.

"But I know you won't take things to the next level if I have another man's child," Olivia wailed. "*Te amo mucho! Eres el amor de mi vida!*"

"Olivia...baby...calm down honey..." Karim begged, feeling terrible about the situation.

Olivia cried hard for what seemed like an eternity before the tears finally subsided. She exhaled loudly.

"I'll call you back later *Papacito*," she whispered.

"Ok baby, I—"

But she had already hung up.

Karim sighed and looked at his lunch. It was now cold. He buzzed Aiesha on the intercom to get it warmed up in the microwave for him. He really felt bad for Olivia but what could he do?

ᴄᴿ...ᴓᴄᴿ...ᴓ

"I think you should go for it," Yanique advised, after listening to Shari tell her about the situation with Karim. "No man has ever had that kind of effect on you. And besides, he's hot, gainfully employed and he wants you bad. You can't put your life on hold because of past experiences Shari. I keep telling you, your boyfriends dying were just strange, twisted coincidences. You had nothing to do with it. I understand that it wasn't easy for you dealing with all that grief but it wasn't your fault. None of it was."

She paused and looked at Shari.

"You deserve to be happy again. Give this guy a chance."

Shari sipped her shake. Everything Yanique said made sense but damn it was difficult to open up to another man again.

She felt eyes on her and looked to her right. A woman was staring at her with a look that she couldn't read. It took Shari a few seconds before she recognized her. It was Zara. Nicholas' ex-girlfriend that had been causing problems before his untimely death. She was lunching with a Caucasian man. There was a scar on her forehead. A souvenir from the accident that had claimed Nicholas' life.

Shari treated her to a dirty look before turning her attention back to Yanique.

Fucking bitch.

"It's hard Yanique...so hard," Shari said before she was rudely interrupted.

"Excuse me," said a testy voice.

Shari looked up. What the fuck did this bitch want with her? She had had a splendid reunion with Nicholas mere hours before he died. She had gotten what she wanted. So why was she speaking to her?

Shari treated her to a hostile gaze.

"Aren't you the girl I met at Nicholas' home the night he died?" she asked, her mouth turned up in a sneer.

Shari was incredulous. The nerve of this slut.

"If you don't want another scar on that ugly face of yours I suggest that you move the fuck away from this table," Shari told her with a deadly calm.

Zara looked at her defiantly, daring her to back up her threat.

Yanique had seen enough. She got up and grabbed Zara by the front of her blouse and pulled her close.

"Are you deaf?" Yanique asked as she shook her like a rag doll before releasing her.

Everyone in the fast food restaurant watched the drama unfold with wide eyes. It wasn't often one saw three well-dressed professional looking women in a fight.

Zara walked away from their table swiftly, going over to her table and snatching up her pocketbook before heading straight out the door. Her date, his white face red with embarrassment, followed.

"Yanique!" Shari exclaimed, laughing. "I can't believe you just did that!"

"Fuck that bitch...she's lucky...if we were in another setting she would have gotten much more than that."

Shari laughed.

That was true.

And the way how she disliked her, she would have definitely joined in.

CR...SOCR...SO

Later that night, Karim was in bed relaxing. He blew out a thin cloud of marijuana smoke. It was some good weed. He was already high and he had just lit the joint. A mixtape with the latest hip hop and R&B releases blared through his state of the art surround sound stereo that was located in the living room. He rhymed along with Uncle Murder, a new rapper out of Brooklyn who was gaining a lot of attention for his slick metaphors and hardcore style.

Shari was on his mind. He wondered how she felt about the orchid that he sent to her. She hadn't contacted him so he didn't know what to think. He was happy that he had decided to plunge ahead and pursue her though. Her reaction to him at the restaurant yesterday had shown him in no uncertain terms that despite her outward coldness to him, she was feeling him big time. Maybe that was the reason she was trying to fight it. It scared her how much she wanted him. Well if she was scared she'd best get a dog as he wasn't going to ease up one bit.

She was going to be his.

End of story.

Chapter 22

The following day, when Shari returned to the office from a meeting up by Manor Park with a real estate firm that she was trying to get some business from, another box was at the front desk waiting for her. Everyone at the office was curious about what was going on. No one there had ever met or seen any of Shari's boyfriends but this seemed like a new one, they had gossiped after seeing two packages come for her two days in a row. They watched while pretending not to as she made her way to her cubicle trying to keep the excitement bubbling inside her petite frame from off her face.

Her conversation with Yanique at lunch yesterday had been helpful but it hadn't been enough to convince her to throw caution to the wind. She sat down and booted up her PC, leaving the box unopened on her desk. Predictably, Danny found a reason to come to her cubicle; asking his lame question that he could have buzzed her on the intercom and asked, while his beady eyes looked at the unopened package disappointedly.

Shari couldn't stand him, though the feeling was mutual. Though apart from the boss, Mr. Carter, and the bearer who ran errands for the company, Danny was the only man, he was the biggest bitch in the company. Shari had never met anyone, male or female, who liked to gossip more than Danny. The staff had never liked her much in the two years that she had been there. She was the youngest one there, cute and very stylish, she didn't like to gossip and she showed them up with her exemplary attitude towards work and her excellent track record since being there. The fact that she was the apple of the boss' eye just made matters worse.

Lately, the cattiness had gotten even worse since she got a raise. Danny, of course, had unprofessionally blabbed to the others that she had gotten a raise despite already being the highest paid employee. Shari didn't give a shit though. She wasn't getting anything that she didn't deserve. They could all kick rocks for all she cared. Besides, for the most part, they all smiled up in her face and tried to be her friend.

Matter of fact, that's how she found out about some of the things that were being said about her.

One of them, Kerry-Ann, the graphic designer, in an attempt to win Shari's confidence, had told her everything. It hadn't worked of course, and she now hated Shari with a passion.

Unable to hold out any longer, Shari finally opened the box. It was long and slender like the one she had gotten yesterday but this one was purple with a white ribbon. Inside was a single purple rose. There was also a card.

A rose is a symbol of love and passion, and a purple rose, in particular, represents enchantment and love at first sight. I now realize that I fell for you the very first time we met. My heart is yours. What are you waiting for to claim it?
Karim

Shari had to smile. She couldn't even front, Karim was doing his thing. The flowers and the way they were presented were off the chain. Goddamn him. She sighed and placed the rose and card back inside the box. How the hell was she supposed to concentrate on work for the rest of the day now?

Thank God it was Friday.

CR...ꞂꝎCR...Ꞃ

Karim arrived at Zenith Marketing and Advertising Agency a few minutes after 5 p.m. He slid into an available parking spot between a blue Honda Civic and a green Nissan Frontier. Shari's vehicle was a few cars down. He had left the office early, having convinced himself that this was the next step. He had to see her and seeing as he didn't know where she lived, he decided to stop by her workplace and fortunately, she was there.

He sat in his truck and waited while he listened to some music.

He watched as a group of employees exited the building. Three women and a man who acted more feminine than all the women combined. They piled into the blue Honda Civic which the man drove, and headed out. Five minutes later, two more women exited and went into a grey Toyota Corolla that was parked next to Shari's truck.

Ten more minutes passed before Shari finally emerged. Karim sucked in his breath. She was so cute and sexy. She had a faraway look on her face as she walked towards her vehicle. She was wearing tight blue jeans which showcased her petite but curvy body and a brown blazer over a dark green top. A pair of trendy brown suede loafers adorned her small feet. He climbed out of the truck and approached her.

She had just deactivated the alarm and was about to enter the vehicle when she turned and saw him. She gasped in surprise.

"Karim! What are you doing here? Are you stalking me?" she asked feigning anger. She was delighted though very disturbed and surprised to see him.

"Yes," he replied simply, as he advanced towards her.

Shari took an involuntary step back.

"Don't come any closer Karim...you need to stop invading my personal space," Shari said as she continued to back up.

"You need to stop playing with me," Karim replied moving faster towards her. Shari turned and ran around the vehicle, feeling like a silly teenager. What was wrong with her? What was it about this man that made her unable to think straight when he was in her presence?

Karim ran her down and held on to her as she tried to go inside the vehicle.

"You think this is a game?" he growled, pressing her against the vehicle.

Shari's knees felt weak. Her poor heart was beating so fast she wondered if it was going to explode. She could feel her center getting moist with alarming speed. He was aroused. His erection shifted against her stomach.

She looked up at him, her light brown eyes glowing with defiance and confusion.

"Who's playing?" she whispered hoarsely, trying to fight the effect his intoxicating nearness was having on her. She still couldn't believe that he had been outside waiting for her and was now pressed up against her, his erection boring a hole in her flat stomach. It was all so surreal. She had been thinking about him and poof, there he was.

He lowered his head and claimed her lips in a gentle but insistent kiss. Shari opened her mouth to protest and he took full advantage, sliding his tongue inside and exploring her depths passionately. Shari moaned and clung to him tightly, kissing him with more passion than she had ever kissed anyone in her entire life, her body succumbing to its destiny, freeing all the demons that had been plaguing her, frustrating her, making her run away from what could be a chance at happiness.

They were both breathless when they finally broke the kiss.

She still clung to him tightly, fearing she would collapse to the ground if she let go. Her knees were about as sturdy as jelly.

"Ahem," a voice said to their right.

It was Mr. Carter.

He was standing there with a bemused expression on his face.

Shari tried to let Karim go but he wasn't having it.

"Hi Mr. Carter," Shari said, completely flustered and embarrassed, her usually pouty lips extra plump from the passionate kiss she had shared with Karim.

"Are you ok?" he asked, feeling very paternal. He felt like he had just caught his own daughter kissing a guy.

"I'm fine...ummm...this is Karim, Karim meet Mr. Carter, my boss," Shari said, remembering her manners.

Karim adjusted himself just enough so that he could shake Mr. Carter's hand.

"Nice to meet you," he said politely, giving Mr. Carter a very firm handshake.

"Ok, I'm heading out now...enjoy the weekend. Young man, take good care of her," he warned with a disarming smile as he entered the Nissan Frontier and drove out.

Their vehicles were the only two that remained in the small parking lot.

They stood looking at each other in a half embrace.

"Karim...my head is spinning...I need to go...I'll call you over the weekend. I promise," she told him, anxious to go before things got out of hand. She needed to think and regroup and she couldn't do that with him around.

He looked at her for a long time before kissing her tenderly on the forehead and releasing her. She smiled at him weakly and got into her vehicle. She then headed out into the Friday evening traffic.

She was crying.

She wasn't sure why.

Chapter 23

At 9 p.m. that night, Karim was at the Tiger Mart on Dunrobin getting a phone card for a friend who had asked him to get her some minutes, when he bumped into Justine. He had just finished paying for the card and was going through the door at the same time she was coming in.

"Hi," Karim said, looking at her surprised. He didn't remember her looking this good. She was wearing a short grey denim skirt, black stilettos and a red top. Not bad at all, especially her legs, but for some reason he just wasn't feeling her.

She stepped back outside to talk to him.

"Hey yourself...why did you take my number if you knew you weren't gonna call me?" she asked, one hand on her hip, whilst the other held a black patent leather Dooney & Burke handbag.

"I had planned to...just didn't get around to it," Karim told her, shrugging his shoulders.

She looked at him steadily, biting her lip. He was looking at her legs. They were her best asset and they were on full display tonight.

"I see...so what are you up to tonight?" she asked, admiring the large tribal tattoo that covered most of the outside of his right hand. He was wearing a dark green Lacoste polo type shirt with shorts and green and white Air Force Ones.

"No major plans...I'm going by one of my friends to hang out for a bit and then I'll see what's up for the rest of the night."

"Well I'm going to hang out with my girls for a few hours...the night is young...maybe we could link up afterwards?" she suggested.

Karim was about to respond when her phone rang. She rummaged through her bag and retrieved it.

"Yes, Shari?" she said.

Karim's entire body reacted when he heard that name.

"I'm coming, damn! I just stopped by the Tiger Mart to get something...I'll be there soon," Justine was saying.

She listened some more and then terminated the call.

"My girlfriend Shari thinks she's the mother hen of the crew...with her short ass," Justine joked, putting the phone back inside her bag.

"What's her last name?" Karim asked.

Justine looked at him quizzically. "Golding. Why?"

Then she remembered that Karim was the guy involved in the car accident with Shari a few months ago.

"Oh, yeah. You do know her. You guys had that fender bender."

Shit! Shit! Shit! Karim thought inwardly. He said a silent prayer to God thanking him that he had not slept with this girl. Shari didn't seem like the kind of girl that would overlook him having been intimate with one of her friends and still get with him. He had seen Shari a couple times with her friends but he hadn't even looked at them. He had only had eyes for Shari.

Karim chuckled and shook his head.

"Yeah I know her...and I really like her," Karim told her.

What! So that's why he hasn't called me!

Justine glared at him.

"You're not Shari's type...sorry to burst your bubble but you're wasting your time," she told him with a sardonic smile. "And besides...you don't really want to go there...every serious boyfriend she has ever had has died a tragic death. Four straight. She has the killer pussy."

She laughed at her own joke as Karim looked at her with disdain. What a bitch. How could she say something like that about her friend?

"*You're* not my type...sorry to burst *your* bubble," Karim told her, watching with satisfaction as her eyes darkened in anger.

"Fuck you!" she told him and walked away, pushing the door angrily as she went inside the Tiger Mart.

Karim shook his head and walked off to his truck. How Shari could stomach having her as a friend was beyond him.

CR...SOCR...SO

"Look who finally decided to show up," Shari commented dryly, as she took a sip of her martini. She and Yanique had been at their favourite Friday night watering hole for over half an hour waiting for Justine to arrive. The place was buzzing with activity. It was happy hour, karaoke was going on and the pool tables were full.

"The queen is here," Justine declared, sitting down on the seat that her friends had saved for her.

"Just sit your tired ass down," Yanique quipped, as Shari laughed.

Justine gave Yanique the 'hand' and called over one of the roaming waiters.

"I'll have what they are having," she told him.

She looked around and her eye caught this guy that she knew. She waved hi and turned her attention back to her friends.

"She's really awful," Shari commented, referring to the young lady who was doing an animated rendition of Whitney Houston's *I Will Always Love You.*

"And ugly," Justine added.

No one laughed. Justine had this really nasty habit of calling everyone ugly.

The waiter came with her drink and she took a big sip.

"Do you guys remember that cute guy we saw at the sports bar on Super Bowl Sunday? The one whose car Shari had damaged?" she asked.

Shari's heart started racing. Her throat suddenly felt dry. She took a sip of her martini.

"Yeah, what about him?" Yanique asked.

Justine sipped her martini before answering.

"I fucked him the other day and he just can't seem to get over it. Keeps pestering me and stuff. I had to tell him off a little while ago when I bumped into him at the Tiger Mart."

Yanique's bulging eyes looked at Shari. Shari looked ill. She was sitting very still.

"What!" Yanique exclaimed.

"Yeah girl," Justine expounded. "It was just a one time thing for me but of course he wanted more. But can you blame the poor guy. He wasn't all that though. Very disappointing. Such a shame that a hot guy like that cannot fuck."

Shari felt like she was going to throw up. She grabbed her pocketbook, excused herself and walked unsteadily towards the bathroom.

Yanique was in shock. If Justine was to be believed the guy was a dog. He had fucked Justine and was now trying to move on to her friend. Poor Shari. She had confided to Yanique a few minutes before Justine arrived that she had decided to give the guy a chance. And now this. It was kind of strange that Justine hadn't mentioned it before though. It wasn't like her to keep things like that to herself. Yanique remembered when Justine had slept with a popular entertainer. She had called them to talk about it the minute she had left the guy's house.

"So how come you're just now telling us?" Yanique asked.

Justine shrugged. "No particular reason. It doesn't matter. What's wrong with Shari?"

Shari had only confided in Yanique about the situation with Karim and she had told Yanique not to say anything about it to Justine.

"I don't know...I'm going to go check on her," Yanique said, getting up.

"Yeah for real," Justine agreed, getting up also.

"No, you stay and watch our drinks," Yanique told her, walking off before she could argue.

"Shari? Shari?" Yanique called out when she got to the bathroom. There were two stalls in there and only one of them was closed.

"Yeah I'm coming," Shari replied in a strained voice.

A few seconds passed and she came out of the stall.

Yanique hugged her.

"Hush...but its better you found out now than later...before you had gotten in deeper with him," Yanique told her.

"It hurts Yanique. I really, really like this guy and he was just playing with me. Fucking with my head. It was all a game to him," Shari sniffed.

"What an asshole...look at the trouble he was going through to get me and he doesn't want me. Just wanted a fuck. That's why I hate little boys. It's my fault. I should have never encouraged him. Fucking shithead," Shari vented.

She broke Yanique's embrace and went by the sink. She cleaned her face and reapplied her make-up. Two giggling girls came inside the bathroom and went into the same stall though the two stalls were unoccupied.

Yanique looked at Shari with her eyebrows arched. Shari smiled weakly, looking at Yanique through the mirror. She just couldn't believe that Karim had turned out to be a sick joke. The bastard. That was one of the main reasons that she didn't date young guys. They played too many games. She was upset at herself for allowing this guy to get inside her head. She knew better. At least she hadn't slept with him. That was some consolation.

She felt a little better as they headed back to the table.

But only a little.

She was very disappointed at the turn of events.
She liked him so much.
Why did he have to be a dog?

Chapter 24

Karim got home at 1 a.m. after hanging out with a few of his friends. He wasn't sleepy but he wasn't really having fun so he had decided to make it a short night. He went to his computer desk and sat down, booting up the computer as he did so. He was thinking about what Shari's friend had said about her. He wondered if it was true. Had all her boyfriends really died under tragic circumstances? That was some crazy shit. Not one but all four? Damn. That must have been very hard for her to deal with. He wondered if that was the reason she was giving him such a hard time. His heart went out to her. The poor girl must have at some point wondered if she was somehow the reason for their deaths. It was only human. Her friend was a real bitch though. Putting her business out there like that. He wouldn't mention it to Shari. When they got together, and he was sure that was going to the case, maybe she would talk to him about it after she was comfortable with him.

He typed in his password and then went on the internet. His phone beeped. He took his Blackberry Curve out of the holster. He had an email from Olivia. He didn't bother to read it on the phone seeing as he was on the computer. He signed into his Yahoo account quickly, anxious to see what she had to say. He had called her a couple times since the last time they spoke but her mobile had rung without an answer. Worried, he had called Taj to find if he had seen her lately and he had said yes, and that she seemed ok but was a bit reserved.

He opened the message.

Papacito. I love you. You are the love of my life. Of that I'm sure. But it's obvious that we are not going to be together. That harsh fact is threatening to drive me loco but I have to deal with it. I'm going to have the baby and try and make things work with the guy. I want my child to have its father around unlike I did. Please don't try to contact me. The only way I can do this is to cut all ties...at least for now. It hurts so bad. Te quiero con todo mi Corazon.

Olivia

Wow. He read the message again before signing out. He was going to miss her, especially with their friendship ending like this. She was everything and a bag of chips and he really, really liked her. He just didn't love her. But everything happened for a reason. He really hoped the guy took good care of her though he knew that Olivia was a strong ambitious girl that could take care of her herself.

He went into the kitchen to get some juice. Shari crossed his mind. He wondered what she was doing.

CR...SOCR...SO

Shari turned off the light and got underneath the covers. The night was finally over. The minute Justine had made her startling admission she had just wanted to go home. And cry. And cry some more. But she had stuck it out, though she was mostly quiet for the rest of the night. She badly wanted to call Karim and give him a piece of her mind. Matter of fact she wanted to slap his face so hard. Bastard. He had hurt her before she had even given in to him.

Shari sighed. Why were some men so evil? How could he go through so much trouble to convince her that he wanted – no *needed* – her in his life if it wasn't real? It just didn't make any sense. And Justine. How come she took so long to mention it when she had literally creamed her panties when they had seen him on Super Bowl Sunday? And the part about Karim not being good in bed, she instinctively knew that was not true. But why would Justine lie? It's not like she knew that Karim was pursuing her. She got up in frustration after tossing and turning for half an hour. She turned on the light and sat up in bed. It was now 2 a.m. Fuck it. Taking a deep breath, she took up her phone and dialed Karim's number. She had to get this off her chest.

He answered on the second ring.

"Hi Shari," he said, sounding wide awake and pleasantly surprised.

Probably thinks that it's a booty call. Fucking prick, Shari fumed inwardly.

"Your game has been exposed, asshole," Shari tore into him right away, feeling better as each syllable left her tongue, abandoning her original plan to at least give him a chance to explain. "Stay the fuck away from me and don't *ever* try to contact me again. I can't believe I almost fell for your bullshit. You need to grow up –"

"What! Shari...what is going on?" Karim broke in, stunned by what she was saying. "I seriously don't know what you're talking about. What game have I been playing with you?"

Shari snorted derisively. "Come on Karim, be a fucking man. Just come clean. Nothing is going to happen between us any way so just keep it real. Have some dignity."

"Shari Golding, please tell me what you are talking about," Karim said calmly, trying valiantly not to let her insults get to him. She was obviously furious about something. He just wished she would tell him what it was. "Please, just tell me."

Shari sighed in frustration.

"Justine," she spat. "She told me everything."

Karim was bewildered. "You're upset because I took her phone number? Shari, I had the number for weeks and never even called her. And I didn't know that you guys were friends. I swear to you."

Shari cackled mirthlessly.

"You must think I'm stupid. Anyways, it's obvious that you are a pathological liar so it makes no sense to continue this conversation. Goodbye Karim. Fuck you and have a nice life."

Shari terminated the call and turned off her phone. She then turned off the light and tried to go to sleep. She had thought that telling him off would have made her feel better but it hadn't.

She felt sad.

Empty.

She hadn't realized how much she had liked him until now, when it really sank in that they would never be together.

ᑫ…ᔐᑫ…ᔐ

Karim was looking at his cell phone like it was the first time he was seeing it. What the fuck just happened? He quickly called her back but it went to voicemail. He left a message.

I'm very disappointed in you Shari. I would never believe in a million years that you would disrespect me like that without even giving me a chance to explain. I seriously don't know what you're so mad about. Justine is obviously at the center of it but whatever she has told you is a lie. How could you give up on us before we even get started based on something somebody else said? That's fucked up but I guess everything happens for a reason.

He threw the phone down on the couch disgustedly. Damn! Just when it seemed like things were finally going to jump off this bullshit had to happen. He wondered exactly what it was that Justine had told Shari. She probably made it seem as though he had slept with her and was now trying to move in on another one in the crew. That made him angry. Very angry. Hell really had no fury like a woman scorned. He didn't want her so she had decided to fuck up his chances of having anything with Shari. Karim decided that he was not going to let her win. Justine was not a good person, not the good friend that Shari thought she was. And he was going to let Shari know that. He would have to wait until next week when Shari went back to work as he didn't know where she lived and he was sure that she wouldn't take his calls.

He sighed in frustration.

This would be the longest weekend of his life.

Chapter 25

Shari sighed as she drove into the parking lot of her workplace at 9 a.m. Monday morning. It had taken every ounce of her willpower to resist the urge to call in sick and get out of bed this morning. The weekend had been terrible. She had practically stayed in bed Saturday and Sunday, eating and watching sports and movies. She had ignored her friends, especially Justine. Maybe it wasn't fair, but she partially blamed Justine for the way her heart was hurting.

She had listened to Karim's message over and over again, the sound of his voice making her heart weep. He was right. She had never given him a chance to explain. She had picked up the phone to call him several times but didn't. She knew it was the right thing to do, to call him back and apologize for not giving him a chance to defend himself. Hell she hadn't even told him everything that Justine had said. She had just ripped into him mercilessly. She felt really bad at her handling of the situation and the pain in his voice when she listened to his message made her feel even worse. Yet, she still hadn't called him back. Shari used to love her stubborn streak but right now it wasn't doing her any good.

"Good morning," Shari said wearily, greeting the bearer who was just leaving to run his morning errands.

She went inside and almost had a heart attack.

Karim was sitting on a chair in the receptionist area.

The receptionist was looking at the two of them with a curious, excited expression.

Shari turned around and went back out the door.

છ... સ્ટછ...સ્ટ

Karim went out after her quickly, fearing that she would jump into her vehicle and drive away.

"Shari, don't go," he said softly when he caught up with her.

She opened her vehicle and placed her stuff on the seat before turning around to face him.

"I'm not leaving," she said hoarsely, her voice choked with emotion. Even after the way she had dealt with him the other day he was still trying. He looked so good, though he seemed a bit tired. "I just don't want anyone in the office all up in my business."

She looked around.

"Where's your truck?" she asked.

Karim smiled sheepishly.

"I paid the security guard at the complex across the street to allow me to park there for an hour. I didn't want you to come and see my vehicle and turn right back."

Shari shook her head sadly.

"I'm terrible...aren't I?"

Karim moved closer to her.

"Stubborn yes, but terrible? Nah...I wouldn't take it that far," Karim replied, smiling a smile that made her heart skip three beats.

"Listen, Karim, I'm really sorry about what happened the other day...I totally went about it the wrong way," she told him.

Karim nodded.

"Yeah...that was crazy. Now tell me exactly what that was all about."

Shari sighed deeply and then told him everything that Justine had said.

Karim listened, his eyes darkening in anger, until she was through.

He used a solitary finger to pull her head up so that she could look at his face.

"I didn't sleep with your friend. She came on to me a few weeks ago at a supermarket and not wanting to embarrass her, I took her number. But I never called her. Yes, she did bump in to me the other night at the Tiger Mart. Matter of fact, that's how your name came up as I was standing in front of her when you called to find out where she was. I told her that I never called because I was really interested in you."

He paused and wiped a tear that had escaped and was running down her right cheek.

"When I told her that, she became angry and cursed me out. Calling me a fool, saying that if it's killer pussy that I want then I should go ahead and fuck you so that I can die. She said that every man that you'd ever been with has died a tragic death."

Shari gasped. She couldn't believe what she was hearing. How could someone who was one of her best friends say such terrible things about her? She was hurt, disappointed, angry and embarrassed. Killer pussy indeed. Justine was such a bitch. She tried to say something but nothing came out.

"Look, baby, I don't care about any of that crap...all I know is that I want us to give this a chance. That's all I'm asking for. Give me a chance to prove to you that we belong together. Fuck the past, fuck whatever happened before...lets live in the now," he said softly but earnestly.

"It's true," Shari whispered, tears streaming down her face freely. "I'm a man killer...I've had four serious boyfriends and they have all passed away...tragically."

Karim was stunned. It really was true. That was some coincidence but he was convinced that's all it was. A coincidence. Shit happens. And sometimes the same shit happens to the same person on more than one occasion. He remembered this girl he knew that had gotten raped three times. And it wasn't anything she had done that had caused it to happen to her once, much less three times. Life was like that sometimes. His grandmother used to say that bad luck was worse than obeah. Shari simply had bad luck when it came to men.

That was about to change.

"I don't care baby, none of it was your fault and I know you're too intelligent to actually believe that you had something to do with their deaths. We're going to grow old together, you'll see," he said, his eyes twinkling.

Shari smiled weakly.

"You're not afraid? You don't think that's weird Karim?"

"Baby it's a crazy coincidence but that's all it was...nothing more, nothing less."

Shari sighed and looked at him. She could see so many things in his eyes: desire, affection, lust, love.

The last one scared her. How could he love her already? But he did. She could see it and feel it. She knew that as soon as she let go and let him inside her body and heart, that she would love him too.

She was done fighting.

She pulled his head down and kissed him, not caring that the assholes in the office were most likely watching through one of the windows.

She kissed him deeply and passionately, giving them their money's worth.

œ...๑œ...๑

"You're in a good mood today," Aiesha remarked when Karim, smiling broadly, entered the office and told her good morning. She handed him his messages.

"Yeah...it's a beautiful day," he replied, humming as he headed down to his office.

She watched him curiously until he was out of her sight. Only one thing could put that kind of smile on a man's face.

Love.

Her boss was in love.

Her heart sank.

Instinctively she knew that it was highly unlikely that he would be intimate with her again. At least not for a long time. The thought saddened her. She wondered who the lucky woman was.

Karim looked at the pile of messages that Aiesha had given to him after he sat down and booted up his computer. He returned two of the more important calls and then checked the office email. He was expecting an important email from a supplier in China. It was there. Great. Everything was going as planned. The items he ordered had been sourced and would arrive in Jamaica in six weeks.

It was really turning out to be a great day.

He was happy that he had decided to go and see Shari this morning. It had taken guts and determination but his mother used to always tell him that anything that's worth having never usually comes easy. So he had put his pride aside and had been beautifully rewarded.

Shari was now his.

After all the roadblocks and problems, she was now his.

That simple fact had had him grinning like an idiot ever since he left her workplace. She had told him that she was going to meet with up Justine later and after that they would spend some time together.

He could only imagine what the conversation between her and Justine was going to be like. He hoped it wouldn't take long.

He couldn't wait to have Shari in his arms.

CR...୨୦CR...୨୦

Shari was pensive as she drove to Yanique's house. She had called both of them immediately after Karim left that morning to request a meeting at Yanique's house at 6 p.m. She felt betrayed and hurt by Justine. So that was what she really believed, what she really thought of her when all this time she was pretending to be supportive and understanding. Killer Pussy. What a name. If it hadn't been used in a malicious way it would have been funny. She got to Yanique's house and parked behind Justine's white Suzuki Swift. She was already there. Good. Shari got out of her vehicle, activated the alarm, and went into the yard. The grill was closed but Yanique saw her through the open front door and let her in.

They hugged and Shari followed her inside.

Justine looked up from the magazine she was leafing through.

"Hey you, what's up? What was so important that I had to break my neck to get here at 6?" she asked.

Shari looked at her with a sad expression. She hated hypocrites. She hated liars. Justine was both. She always knew that Justine could be a bitch but they had all been close despite that. At least she wasn't a bitch to them. Or so she had thought.

"Yeah what's up Shari?" Yanique asked, anxious to know as well. Shari had refused to say over the phone no matter how she had begged.

Shari sat down and crossed her legs. She looked at Justine.

"That's a cute nickname you have for me," she said dryly.

Justine screwed up her face in consternation. "What are you talking about?"

"Killer pussy. Wasn't that the name you called me when Karim told you that he was interested in me?" Shari asked, watching as her expression moved from being puzzled to being surprised before settling on being defensive.

Yanique looked at Justine with disdain but she didn't say anything. This was Shari's moment.

"Yeah I said it...what's the big deal? Isn't it true?" she said, ashamed that she had been found out but deciding to take the I-don't-give-a-fuck-route.

"The only thing that's true is that you're a hypocrite and a liar. Two very despicable things to be. You should be ashamed of yourself, talking about one of your so-called best friends like that behind her back just because the man that you were throwing yourself at didn't want you but wanted her instead," Shari replied calmly. "I actually feel sorry for you. You have been envious of me from the day we met. I really shouldn't be too surprised that you would stoop this low."

Justine got up from the chair suddenly, her face twisted in anger.

"Envious of you? Bitch please! Get over yourself," she retorted.

"We are no longer friends Justine. It's a wrap. And do remember, you can pay for school but you can't buy class," Shari told her, getting up as well.

"I'll speak with you later Yanique," Shari said, "My man is waiting on me."

She looked at Justine liked she was road kill and made her exit. They could hear her vehicle driving off a few seconds later.

Yanique hadn't said anything all this time and she still didn't. She just sat there and looked at Justine.

Justine looked like she was about to say something, changed her mind, grabbed her handbag and left.

Yanique got up and closed the grill and front door.

So that was that.

The three musketeers had become two.

Chapter 26

Karim arrived at Shari's apartment at 8 p.m. He couldn't believe how nervous and excited he was. That was not a familiar feeling women usually brought out in him, at least not the nervous part. He was finally going to spend some time with her. Alone. It wasn't a given that they would have sex but he was prepared. A pack of Trojan Magnums was in the pocket of the slim fit Affliction hooded sweatshirt that he was wearing. But it didn't matter whether they had sex tonight or not. He was just happy to be here.

He went up to her apartment door and knocked.

She opened the door after a few seconds, removing the chain and allowing him to come in.

But he didn't.

He stood there for a few moments, admiring her.

She was wearing a sheer white negligee. Nothing was underneath.

Shari's body temperature rose under his intense gaze. At first she had thought that her outfit would be too daring, too forward and revealing for his very first visit to her home but fuck that.

He was now her man.

And she had wasted enough time denying him.

Denying her.

Denying them.

If the eyes were mirrors to the soul then Karim's soul was in an erotic turmoil of unbridled lust and desire.

Shari felt weak.

She needed to feel him inside her more than how the American economy needed a stimulus package.

He finally stepped in and she closed the door behind him.

She moved into his arms.

"Hi baby," he said, hugging her tightly.

"Mmmm," she moaned. "I feel so safe and wanted in your arms."

Karim smiled.

"What's that sticking me honey?" she asked huskily, feeling something very hard pressing into her stomach. She remembered the day that he had hugged and kissed her in the parking lot at her workplace. His dick had probed her stomach then, just as it was doing now. Difference was, this time she could do something about it.

Her pussy knew the difference too.

It was so wet that Shari figured that she would have to drink a lot of fluids later when they were through to replenish her body.

"Your dick," Karim whispered hoarsely as she caressed it through his jeans.

"Really...." Shari breathed as she unbuckled his jeans and dropped them to his ankles.

His boxers followed swiftly.

"It's beautiful Karim," she said.

Karim laughed.

"It's true...perfect size...nice complexion...it even has a mole," Shari told him, grinning. "Now let me see if it tastes as good as it looks."

Karim pulled off his sweatshirt and undershirt as he felt her hot mouth envelope the head of his dick.

"Baby...mmmm....oh God baby..." Karim moaned, standing with his legs as wide as the jeans bunched around his ankles would allow, with his back slightly hunched.

"Mmmmm....taste so fucking good baby...my dick taste so fucking good...so good....mmmm...." Shari breathed between slurps as she sucked him languidly, savouring the feel and taste of his perfectly proportioned tool in her mouth.

Just when he thought that his knees would give way from pleasure if he continued to stand much longer, Shari finally raised her head, stopping long enough for him to remove his sneakers and jeans. She admired him from her vantage point, crouched on the floor. He was now naked with just his ankle socks on. He had a gorgeous body. Firm and defined without looking like he lived in the gym. Just looked like a naturally blessed man who took care of himself well enough. His thighs looked powerful, like he did track. She could just imagine the force with which they would be helping to propel his dick up inside her.

She almost climaxed from the image.

She rose unsteadily and slipped off her negligee.

Karim groaned and lifted her like a rag doll, turning her upside down in the air, and still standing and holding her by the waist, buried his face inside her pussy.

"Oh my fucking God!" Shari shrieked, feeling dizzy as he assaulted her pussy with what had to be a battery operated tongue, as all the blood rushed to her head from being suspended in the air upside down. His dick bobbed in front of her face. She stroked and sucked it intermittently, pausing ever so often to cry out with pleasure.

"My baby! My baby! You're going to make me come so hard! Oh my baby! Right there! You're juicing your pussy so good baby! It's coming for you baby! Right! Fucking! Now! Ohhhhhh!"

Shari shook in his hands mightily and he held on to her tightly as her sweet juices gushed in his mouth in copious amounts, her ass cheeks vibrating against his forehead from the intensity of her climax.

Without missing a beat, Karim turned her around effortlessly and using one hand, guided his shaft inside her wetness. It was like his dick had eyes. It found her pleasure spots easily, hitting them with precision over and over again.

Shari lost her mind.

She didn't even care that he wasn't wearing a condom.

Nothing mattered at this moment.

Karim had her trapped in an erotic asylum where the pleasure was so intense that you were happy to be crazy.

"Jesus Christ! Oh baby! Fuck! I feel it in my chest!" Shari shouted as Karim, walking around the living room with her, raised her high and slammed her down on his rigid shaft over and over again. "Forgive me for giving you so much trouble baby! Punish me for it baby! Punish me! Yes baby! Just like that!"

"I can't be coming again so soon!" Shari said in disbelief as she felt her pelvic area tighten and her pussy flooded his dick once again. "Ohhhh! Ohhhhh! Fuck! Fuck! Fucckkk!"

She wrapped her legs around him tightly and buried her tongue in his mouth as she had the most intense orgasm she had ever experienced in her life. Her pussy felt like it was filled with molten lava.

She continued to kiss him as her orgasm went on and on, draining her body of its precious nutrients.

Tears flowed freely as she kissed him and shuddered in his arms, feeling his dick pulsing inside her ridiculous wetness.

He had just made her completely his.

Had staked his claim on her mind, body and soul.

They were now one.

Karim, looking over her shoulder, walked with her, his embedded dick moving inside her with each step, to the bedroom where he placed her on the edge of the bed and tucked her ankles behind her ears.

Shari saw stars when he began to stroke her hard and deep.

"Oh God baby! It's going to come through my mouth! It hurts baby! It hurts so fucking good! Fuck your pussy baby! I don't care if you kill me! Fuck your pussy! Oh sweet Jesus of Nazareth. I'm coming again!"

Shari fainted during her next orgasm.

Karim, his dick still inside her, slapped her face three times and she came to, looking at him in wonder, delirious from her intense multiple orgasms, wondering if she'd be able to walk when he was through with her.

"What just happened boo?" she asked, feeling like she was having an out of body experience.

"You lost consciousness for a few seconds," he told her, looking down at her plump pussy, which despite its wetness, had his dick in a vice grip.

"Oh my God...that's crazy," Shari breathed. A man had fucked her so good that she had actually fainted from pleasure.

Unbelievable.

And he was her man.

A man that she had almost allowed to get away from her.

She looked up at his handsome face, sweaty from his exertions, and shuddered at the thought.

"I want you to come in my mouth baby...I want to swallow your kids," she told him, her eyes still sparkling with wonder.

Karim growled and resumed stroking her, his tempo increasing with each stroke.

"Yes! Yesss! Yessss! Come for me baby! Give me my fucking vitamins! Give them to me!" Shari urged, slapping his ass like a maniac.

"Ahhhhh! Ahhhhh! Fuck!" Karim shouted as he pulled out of her and Shari quickly got up and opened wide as he shoved his dick inside her mouth and deposited the sweetest tasting semen she had ever had down her throat, his body shaking like the temperature in the bedroom was below zero.

"Oh baby...oh baby...oh baby..." Karim whispered like a broken record as Shari swallowed every drop and continued to suck him until he had to push her away, his nerves frayed.

Shari grinned and staggered to the bathroom like a drunken partygoer to clean up.

Karim stretched out on the bed and watched her in the bathroom. She did not close the door, already so comfortable with him. She was sitting on the toilet. She felt his eyes and smiled at him tiredly. That had been incredible. The first time that he had had sex with someone that he knew he loved. It had been a mind blowing experience. She wiped, flushed and then went over to the sink to brush her teeth.

She was so sexy. Petite, no excess fat – except on her pussy – yet curvy and not skinny. Perfect for him. He loved her bow legs and the way her plump pussy just filled the space between them. He loved her breasts too. Slightly more than a handful and very firm. She finished up and joined him in bed.

"That was indescribable baby," she murmured contentedly, lying on his chest. She wondered how she would get up for work tomorrow. She was *so* tired. Karim had fucked her senseless.

"Damn...it was off the chain baby...best... most intense sex I've ever had," he responded, bending his head to kiss her on the forehead.

She had fallen asleep.

He smiled and hugged her.

He doubted that he was ever happier in his life than he was right at that moment.

He was still smiling when he too, fell asleep.

Epilogue

Karim turned off the light and Shari held on to him as they made their way through the semi-darkness to the bedroom. They had been together for eight months now and the relationship had moved from strength to strength. On Shari's suggestion, Karim had rented out his apartment and had been living with her for the past three months. She had pointed out that people needed to live together for awhile to find out of they could live with each other's dirty habits that didn't usually come to light unless you shared the same roof.

So far it had been great. They complemented each other well. They were both neat, so cleanliness wasn't a problem, they both had their own money plus the joint savings account that they had started four months ago, they both had their own vehicles and they pretty much liked to watch the same things on T.V. The only thing that had taken some getting used to was Karim's smoking. But she had and it wasn't an issue. They had compromised and he didn't smoke inside the house while they had the AC on.

The T-Shirt line that Karim owned with Taj had become really popular and had expanded to include sleepwear and underwear. The line was available in several major retail chains in the US and was available exclusively at their flagship store in Jamaica, which they had opened two months ago.

Olivia had stayed true to her word and had not contacted him. Taj had told Karim that she was now living with the guy and he had not seen her in ages. Taj and Alondra were still together and were now engaged.

Kimberly was now married to a much older man and lived in Philadelphia but she still hadn't gotten over Karim. She still sent him messages by email every now and then, alternately begging to see him and cursing him out.

Shari and Yanique never spoke to Justine again after that meeting at Yanique's house over eight months ago. They saw her out and about with her new friends every now and then but she wisely kept her distance.

Ms. Golding?

Yes? This is she.

I have some terrible news. Your boyfriend, Karim Dawkins was shot and killed by a lone gunman in an attempted carjacking this evening in New Kingston.

No! No! It can't be!

"Baby, baby, wake up," Karim said, switching on the bedside lamp.

Shari was having a nightmare about him dying. She had them every now and then. It didn't faze him and as time went on, he was sure that the nightmares would eventually stop.

She woke up and looked at him with frightened, tear-filled eyes which slowly regained focus when she realized it wasn't real.

"I love you baby," she said, kissing him.

He rubbed her stomach.

"I love you too pookie...and little pookie," he said smiling.

She covered his hand with hers.

She was seven weeks pregnant.

She was going to have his baby.

And there was no way God would take away Karim from their lives. She wasn't too worried about the nightmares. They had to stop at some point.

She had faith.

Faith in life.

Faith in love.

Faith in God.

Everything was going to be alright.

It had to be.

The alternative was unthinkable.

OTHER K. SEAN HARRIS TITLES:

Novels

- The Garrison
- The Heart Collector
- Death Incarnate
- The Stud
- The Stud II
- Merchants of Death: A Jamaican Saga of Drugs, Sex, Violence and Corruption

CR...൭CR...൭

Anthologies

- The Sex Files
- The Sex Files II
- Erotic Jamaican Tales
- More Erotic Jamaican Tales

Breinigsville, PA USA
27 January 2011
254281BV00001B/1/P